Alice in Deadland

Mainak Dhar

DEDICATION

As always, for Puja & Aadi.

ONE

ALICE WAS BEGINNING TO GET very tired of sitting by her sister on the hill, and of having no Biters to shoot. Once or twice she peeped through her sniper rifle's scope, but could see no targets. 'What is the use of an ambush', thought Alice, 'without any Biters to shoot in the head?'

Alice was fifteen, and had been born just three months after The Rising. Her older sister and parents sometimes talked of how the world had been before. They talked of going to the movies, of watching TV, of taking long drives in the countryside, of school. Alice could relate to none of that. The only life she had known was one of hiding from the Biters. The only education that she knew to be useful consisted of three simple lessons - if a Biter bites you, you will become one of them; if a Biter bites someone you know, it doesn't matter whether that person was your best friend, they were now a Biter and would rip your throat out in a heartbeat; and if you could take only one shot, aim for the head. Only the head. Nothing else would put a Biter down for good.

So here she was, lying on a small hillock, her rifle at her shoulder, waiting to pick off any stragglers who escaped the main force. The first few years of her life had been one of hiding, and of surviving from one day to another. But then the humans had begun to regroup and fight back, and the world had been engulfed in a never-ending war between the living and the undead. Alice's parents were part of the main assault force that was now sweeping through a group of Biters that had been spotted near their settlement. She could hear the occasional pop of guns firing, but so far no Biters had come their way. Her sister was lying quietly, as always obedient and somber. Alice could not imagine just lying here, getting bored when the action was elsewhere, so she crawled away to the edge of the small hill they were on and peered through her scope, trying to get a glimpse of the action.

That's when she saw him. The Biter was wearing pink bunny ears of all things. That in itself did not strike Alice as strange. When someone was bitten and joined the undead, they just continued to wear what they had been wearing when they were turned. Perhaps this one had been at a party when he had been bitten. The first Biter she had shot had been wearing a tattered Santa Claus suit. Unlike kids before The Rising, she had not needed her parents to gently break the news that Santa Claus was not real. What was truly peculiar about this Biter was that he was not meandering about mindlessly but seemed to be looking for something. The Biters were supposed to be mindless creatures, possessed of no intelligence other than an overpowering hunger to bite the living. She braced herself, centering the crosshairs of her scope on the Biter's head. He was a good two hundred meters away and moving fast, so it was hardly going to be an easy shot.

That's when the Biter with the bunny ears dropped straight into the ground.

Alice looked on, transfixed, and then without thinking of what she was getting into, ran towards the point where the Biter had seemingly been swallowed up by the ground. Her heart was pounding as she came closer. For months there had been rumors that the Biters had created huge, underground bases where they hid and from which they emerged to wreak havoc. There were stories of entire human armies being destroyed by Biters who suddenly materialized out from the ground and then disappeared. However, nobody had yet found such a base and these stories were largely dismissed as being little more than fanciful fairy tales. Had Alice managed to find such a base?

Her excitement got the better of her caution, and she ran on alone. She should have alerted her sister, she should have called for reinforcements, she should have done a lot of things. But at that moment, all she remembered was where the Biter had dropped into the ground and of what would happen if she had truly found an underground Biter base. She was an excellent shot, far better than most of the adults in the settlement, and she was fast. If there was one thing she had been told by all her teachers since she started training, it was that she was a born fighter. She could put a man twice her size on the mat in the wink of an eye, and she had shown her mettle in numerous skirmishes against the Biters. Yet, she was not allowed to lead raids far from the settlement. That had always grated, but with her father being one of the leaders of the settlement, she was unable to do anything to change that. He claimed that her excellent shooting and scouting skills were better used in defensive roles close to their settlement, and had promised her that when she was older he would reconsider, but she knew that was a nervous father speaking, not the leader of their settlement.

This could change all that.

Suddenly she felt the ground give way under her and she felt herself falling. She managed to hold onto her rifle, but found herself sliding down a smooth, steep and curving slope. There seemed to be no handholds or footholds for her to slow her descent or to try and climb back up. She looked up to see the hole through which light was streaming in disappear as the tunnel she was falling down curved and twisted.

Alice screamed as she continued falling in utter darkness.

~ * * * ~

It took Alice a few minutes to get her bearings, as she was totally disoriented in the dark and also winded by her fall. She saw that her fall had been broken by a thick cushioning of branches and leaves. She had heard whispers that the Biters were not the mindless drones that many adults dismissed them to be, but those accounts had been dismissed by most people as fanciful tales. She wondered if there was some truth to those rumors after all. As her eyes adjusted to the darkness she saw a sliver of light to her right and crawled towards it. As she went deeper into the tunnel, while she still could not see much, the smell was unmistakable. The rotten stench that she knew came from only one possible source- the decayed bodies of the undead. Even though she had seen the aftermath of many a skirmish with the Biters, and was no stranger to the stench, she found herself gagging. As she came closer to the light, she saw that the tunnel opened into a small room that was lit by crudely fashioned torches hung on the walls.

She could hear some voices and as she peeped around the corner, she saw that the rabbit-eared Biter she had followed down was in animated conversation with two others. One of them was, or rather had been in life, perhaps a striking young woman. Now her skin was yellowing and decayed and hung in loose patches on her face. Her clothes were tattered and bloodied.

4

The other Biter with her was a plump, short man who seemed to have the better part of his left side torn off, perhaps by a mine or a grenade. Alice had been around weapons for as long as she could remember, and while all humans now needed to be able to defend themselves, Alice had shown a special talent for fighting, perhaps one her mother did not always approve of. Her mother had wanted Alice to do as the other young people did and stand on guard duty close to the settlements, but Alice had always wanted to be in the forefront, to feel the thrill that came with it. Now, Alice thought, she had perhaps got more thrills than she had ever bargained for. She was trapped in an underground Biter base, with no apparent way out.

The Biters were talking in a mixture of growls and moans, but they seemed to be communicating with each other. Now that she got a closer look at the rabbit-eared Biter she had followed in, she realized that he had been in life not much older than her. Perhaps he had been on his way to a costume party when he had been bitten. As he turned his head, Alice saw what may have once been a smile now replaced by a feral grin that revealed bloodied teeth.

Alice's heart stopped as Bunny Ears looked straight at her. For a second she hoped that he had not seen her, but he bared his teeth and emitted a screeching howl that sent a shiver up her spine. As all three Biters turned to look at her, she exploded into action.

Alice's grasp of the alphabet may have been tenuous despite her mother's many failed attempts to teach her the languages of yore. But after The Rising, Alice saw no use for them- there were no books to read, and no time to read them even if they had remained. But what Alice excelled in school at, and could do almost without conscious thought, was how to thumb the safety off her handgun and bring it up to a two handed hold within three seconds. The first shot took the fat Biter squarely in the forehead and he went down with an unceremonious flop. As the two others bore down on her in the slight loping, lumbering gait the Biters were known for, she fired again and again, the shots from her gun echoing in the underground cavern. She hit the female Biter at least twice in the chest and then knocked her flat with a head shot. Bunny Ears was now barely a few feet away when Alice's handgun clicked empty. She cursed under her breath at her horrible aim, realizing just how much easier it was to shoot at targets in practice or snipe from hundreds of meters away compared to being so close to Biters out for her blood, and with her heart hammering so fast she could barely keep her hands straight, let alone aim.

Alice heard footsteps and howls behind her, and realized with a stab of panic that she was now well and truly trapped between Bunny Ears and others who may have come behind her down the hole.

She looked around frantically and saw a small opening in the wall to her right. She ran towards Bunny Ears, diving down at the last minute beneath his outstretched fingers that were crusted over with dried blood. Alice stood only about five feet tall, and was lean, but she had been top of her class in unarmed combat. She swept her legs under the Biter, coming up in one seamless motion as Bunny Ears fell down in a heap. She ran towards the hole in the wall and turned around to see at least four more Biters coming behind her.

Alice fumbled at her belt and took the lone flash bang grenade she had slung there. As she ran into the hole she pulled the pin and rolled it on the ground behind her, and then continued to run at full speed into the darkness of the hole. She heard the thump of the grenade a few seconds later, hoping that the intense flash of light it emitted would slow down her pursuers for a few seconds and buy her some time.

6

With that hope came a sobering thought. Time to do what? She was stuck deep inside what seemed to be a Biter base, and was running ever deeper into its recesses. She was well and truly trapped.

~ * * * ~

Alice ran till she was out of breath and stopped, going down on her knees, more tired and scared than she had ever been. The darkness and narrowness of the passage she was in did not help, as it made her feel disoriented and claustrophobic. At least she could no longer hear footsteps behind her. That did not surprise her. While the flash bang would not stop the Biters, she knew they hated very bright light, and it would certainly have slowed them down. Also, she was a very fit young girl who could outrun most of the people in their settlement, whereas the Biters pursuing her, while feared for their feral violence, moved with their characteristic stiff, loping gait, which meant she would be able to outrun them in any flat out race. The problem was that she was trapped in their base, and all they had to do was to tire her out.

When she thought she heard distant footsteps behind her, her fear gave her a second wind and she started running again, clutching her side, which had begun to hurt from the exertion. She ran into a wall, and fell back hard on her back, realizing that the tunnel turned ahead of her. As she looked past the turning, she saw what appeared to be a door framed by light coming from behind it. She ran towards it, and as she came closer, she was stunned to see a familiar figure drawn on the door. It was a seal showing an eagle framed by letters that were barely visible in the light coming from behind it. She started trying to read the letters and got past the U, N and I before she realized she did not need to tax her limited reading skills to understand what it showed. She had seen a similar seal in old papers her father kept locked away in a dusty box. Once he had told her something about him having worked in the United States Embassy in New Delhi before The Rising. She had understood little of what he had meant, though other kids around the settlement had told her that her father had been some sort of important man in the governments of the Old World. They had told her that she and her family had come from another land called America, which was why her blond hair and fair skin looked so different from her brown friends. But none of that mattered much to Alice, or to anyone else anymore. The old governments and countries were long gone. Now all people, irrespective of their old countries, religions or politics were bound together in but one overriding compact- the need to survive in the face of the Biter hordes. She had heard tales of how human nations had waged wars against each other, driven by the Gods they worshipped, or the desire to grab oil. Alice remembered laughing when her teacher at the makeshift school in the settlement had told her class about those days. She had thought her teacher was telling them some tall tales. What was it the old folks called them? The ones who had read the books before the undead rose and the world burned.

Yes, fairy tales.

When Alice heard footsteps behind her, she was snapped back to reality, and she struggled with the door in front of her, trying desperately to open it. She found a handle and pulled it with all her strength, and finally found the door budging. The door was made of heavy metal, and it sapped all her strength to open it enough for her to slip through. She looked back through the open door and heard the roars before she saw shadows appear in the tunnel. She pulled the door shut, hoping that what she had heard about Biters being stupid was right. That old joke about how many Biters it took to open a door.

She took a look around the room she was in and saw that it was lit by a single small kerosene lamp on the ceiling, and was filled with papers and files that crammed the shelves lining the walls. There was a small desk in a corner and when she walked to it, she saw some old newspapers on it. She had never seen a newspaper in her life, and was fascinated by the pictures and words she saw. She didn't need to read the words to know what they showed. They were relics of the last days during The Rising and its aftermath. There were grainy pictures of the first appearances of the undead, which she imagined for those who had never seen before them must have been quite a sight. Then there were pictures of burnt and charred cities- the remains of the Great Fire that ` the human governments had unleashed on so many cities when it seemed like all was lost. That was the barren, bleak landscape that Alice had known as home- the wastelands outside New Delhi, where millions had died in the Biter outbreak and then millions more as governments tried to contain the outbreak by using nuclear weapons on the key outbreak centers. Man had proven to be the most jealous of lovers, preferring to destroy the Earth rather than give her up. But it had not been enough, and in the fires of that apocalypse was born a renewed struggle for survival between humans and the undead in the wasteland that was now known simply as the Deadland.

Alice had been so transfixed by what she saw that she had forgotten all about securing the other doors to the room, and she screamed in agony when she realized that there was another door, partially obscured by a chair, which was ajar. She heard footsteps behind it, and realized that what she was taken for escape was in fact nothing more than a death trap.

She took out her handgun from her belt and as she felt for the safety, remembered with dismay that in all the chaos she had forgotten to reload. As she saw shadows enter the door, she realized she had no time for that any more. She unslung the sniper rifle from her shoulders. As such close quarters, there was no hope of her putting it to much use as a long range weapon, but there were other ways to make it count.

As a child, Alice had forever been getting into scrapes, and her parents would never tire of telling her to back down once in a while, instead of wading into every fight. But once after she had shot two Biters during a night-time raid, her father had got quite drunk to celebrate and told her that he loved her spirit and that no matter what the odds, she should never give into fear. To be afraid in the face of the undead was to die, or worse, to become one of *them.*

As Alice remembered her father's words, she felt her fear slip away. She knew that the Biters tried to bite and turn every human they found, but also that the humans who fought back the hardest sometimes enraged them so much that they ripped them apart, killing them instead of turning them into the undead.

Better dead than undead.

That had been the motto of the school where they had been taught survival and combat skills. Whereas little girls before The Rising may have been playing with their toys or watching TV, Alice had grown up playing with guns, explosives and learning the best way to destroy the undead. And she had been the best in her class.

She was now swinging the rifle in front of her like a staff, moving it around her fingers so it cut sharp circles through the air. Three Biters came in, and as the first reached for her, she cracked him across the forehead and leaned toward him, sweeping his legs under him as he went down. The next up was a squat woman wearing the tattered, bloody remains of a saree, and incongruously enough, a huge diamond solitaire earring on her left ear. The right ear was missing. Alice delivered a roundhouse kick that sent Ms. Solitaire stumbling back and then reversed the sniper rifle in her hand, firing a single shot that disintegrated the Biter's head. The third Biter, a tall man with his jaw missing, was almost upon her when she hit him hard in the face with the butt of her rifle. Biters might feel no pain, but it unbalanced him enough for Alice to jump back a few steps and put another round into his chest. Only a head shot would put down a Biter for good, but a high powered sniper rifle bullet did impressive enough damage and slowed one down no matter where it hit. A gaping hole opened in the Biter's chest as he slumped back. Alice knew he'd be at her throat soon enough so she tried to chamber another round in her rifle.

That was when she felt her right arm caught in a cold, clammy grip that was so strong she screamed and dropped her rifle. Bunny Ears was back and he was bringing his face back to bite her arm. Alice kicked him in the shin, but he did not even wince as he came closer to delivering the bite that would be the last thing Alice felt before she became one of *them.*

Alice did the last thing he perhaps expected. She head-butted him and as he staggered back and loosened his grip on her arm, she vaulted over the desk and stood with her back to the wall. There were now no less than six Biters gathered in front of her, and Alice suppressed the welling panic within as she unsheathed the curved hunting knife that was always by her side. Bunny Ears snarled and screamed in rage, a hellish concerto that was soon taken up by all the Biters in the room. Alice had heard of this ritual before. It meant the Biters were going to rip some human apart instead of trying to convert them. Alice reversed the knife in her right hand and stood with her legs slightly spread apart, just as she had mastered in countless hours of unarmed combat practice. Her teacher there had been some sort of elite commando in the armies of the old governments, and he had told her she was his best student. She slowed her breathing, focusing on the creatures in front of her, trying to block out her fear, trying to still her mind. As Bunny Ears stepped toward her, she gripped the knife handle tight and readied herself. Better dead than undead.

TWO

WHEN BUNNY EARS LUNGED AT her, he was met with a sharp kick that had him rocking on his heels and then Alice delivered a knife thrust to his chest. He just looked up and snarled through bloodied teeth before Alice kicked him again, sending him down on one knee. Alice knew it was a losing battle. She was hopelessly outnumbered and even if by some miracle she managed to drive the knife through one of the Biter's brains, that would still leave several of them to rip her apart. Be that as it may, she was not about to go down without a fight. A Biter with half his face torn off reached towards her with a hand that had several fingers missing. Alice put all her strength into it and drove the knife through his skull. The Biter fell back and did not get back up.

Now she had no weapon to defend herself with.

As two more Biters reached towards her, Alice overturned the desk in front of her, sending both of them sprawling, but she knew that at best she was merely delaying the inevitable. She felt a painful blow to the side of her head as Bunny Ears hit her and she fell over hard against the wall.

As she scrambled to get up, she felt cold hands grip

her legs and sharp nails dig into her jeans. She grabbed onto the bookshelf by her side and it toppled over with a crash, scattering papers and files all around her. She was now being dragged along the ground, and could hear the Biters screeching in anticipation of the kill, like a pack of wild dogs around their prey.

Alice looked up to see Bunny Ears looming over her, his eyes yellowed and wide, his skin peeling off in places and his stench unbearable as he bent over her.

Then he suddenly stopped. A couple of the other Biters tried to get to her, but he stopped them with an authoritative roar. Alice cringed as he grabbed her hair, but instead of attacking her, he seemed to be examining it, turning it around in his fingers. Alice was nearly paralyzed with fear, wondering what torture he had in mind for her, half wishing that he would just get it over with and grant her a quick death. As far as she had ever imagined Biters capable of emotions, she saw a flicker of doubt cross Bunny Ear's face, and something had clearly caused him to put his bloodlust on hold. Whatever that was seemed to be something right behind Alice since he seemed to be looking beyond her at the wall where the bookshelf had been seconds earlier.

He reached out with a torn and callused finger and Alice cringed, only to find that he was reaching for the wall behind her. The other Biters were now gathered around him, looking at her. A few of them were jostling and pushing, eager to get at her, but he snarled again, and they held back. Clearly Bunny Ears was in charge here. Whether that was a good thing or not was something Alice reckoned she would find out very soon. He grabbed her hair again, this time almost yanking them out from the roots, and Alice shouted. That got him focused on her again, and he brought his face close to hers. Alice tried hard not to throw up as she smelt his stench and saw his torn and decayed face up close. He was but a few inches away from her face when to her shock he said one word.

'A...a......lissssssssss.'

Alice thought she had imagined it but when he repeated himself, she recoiled in horror. Not only did this creature speak but it was calling out her name. She had not said anything, but her reaction must have given her away. Bunny Ears leapt back, as if he had been electrocuted, and the other Biters all took a step back. She was alone, unarmed and utterly at their mercy, but the tables had somehow been turned in an instant. They seemed to be terrified of her. No, as Alice studied them almost bowing down before her and heard a few more of them growling, trying to utter her name, she realized it was not just fear. They were in awe of her.

Alice scrambled to her feet, unsure of what was going on, when Bunny Ears pointed to the wall behind her. Now that she had got her first close look at Biters outside of the heat of battle when all that mattered was killing them or being bitten, she realized that while they certainly looked hideous and were capable of savage violence, they were also capable of some level of rational action. She hoped that if she did as they wanted, she had at least some chance of appealing to that part of them and getting out alive. As she turned towards the wall, it felt as if the world had stopped around her. On the wall was a drawing, with smudged lines and crudely filled colors, as if it had been made by a small child. But what it showed was clear enough.

It showed a blonde girl jumping down a hole. In front of her was a creature that was wearing some sort of coat but had the unmistakable ears and whiskers of a rabbit. Just above the drawing was etched in a childish scrawl.

'Alice.'

Alice's reading skills may not have been great but

one thing she did know well was how her own name was spelt. She sat down on the ground, oblivious to the bloodthirsty Biters just feet away from her.

What was going on?

She felt strong hands grab her by her shoulders and pull her upright. The Biters were now in a state of considerable agitation and between grunts and screeches, Bunny Ears was trying to tell them something. Whatever it was, they seemed to agree on it soon enough, and Alice was pushed out of the room and into another tunnel.

She was too shell-shocked to resist or even ask where they were taking her. And so Alice was bundled off even deeper into the Biter base.

~ * * * ~

They continued in darkness and total silence for many minutes, and the only consolation Alice had was that if the Biters had wanted to kill her they would have done so long ago. They clearly wanted her alive, but to what end she had no idea. They soon began a steep climb and while the Biters seemed accustomed to both the darkness and the area they were going through, Alice found herself stumbling and falling more than once. Finally they rounded a turn and she felt hands holding her back as if asking her to wait. She saw a sliver of light open up ahead, gradually growing as the door out of the tunnel was pushed open. As she came closer, she saw that it was not much of a door but branches and twigs gathered together, which were now being pushed back into place as their group came out of the tunnel.

The bright sunlight hurt her eyes after having been in the dark for so long and as Alice squinted and looked around, she saw that they were now very much in the heart of what had once been the bustling city of New Delhi. Now all that remained was rubble, but she recognized the broken edifice of what had once been some monument called India Gate. She had only heard about it from the adults, since this was an area that was firmly under the control of the Biters, and was avoided by humans. All around her, she saw evidence of that. There were small groups of Biters lumbering around, and when one or two of them saw her, they snarled and were about to launch themselves at her. Bunny Ears swatted one of them away, and growled a warning to the others. Whatever he said, she realized that her name had been mentioned more than once, and the effect on the Biters was immediate. They all backed away, as if fearful of her, and she continued with the group that was now herding her along to their unknown destination.

Alice subconsciously tried not to breathe too deeply. While the Great Fires had taken place years ago, nobody really knew how much radiation still lingered. When Alice had first heard of the Great Fires and the terrible weapons that had been unleashed, she had wondered aloud how much of the Biters' hideous nature was the result of the radioactive fallout and how much was due to whatever had caused The Rising in the first place. Nobody seemed to have much by way of answers. Most of the nuclear blasts had supposedly been air-bursts designed to incinerate the Biters but keep the ground as free from radiation as possible, but nobody could really be sure what their legacy had been. Her father had by all accounts been someone senior in the Embassy, but things had moved so fast that even he had no real idea of what had been the exact chain of events during the last days.

Alice saw that they were headed towards what seemed to be an opening in the ground. Clearly the rumors about the underground bases had been an understatement. Far from being an isolated base that she had stumbled upon, it seemed like the Biters had a fairly sophisticated network of underground tunnels and bases. She filed away all the details she could spot so that she might be able to help others when she got back. That kept her thinking positively that she would indeed somehow make it back and also took her mind off the growing fear about just where she was being taken.

She heard a dull whirring sound coming from the sky above and she froze. She had heard similar sounds before, and in the past they had always been an unwelcome omen. Today, they signaled hope for her liberation. Bunny Ears pushed her behind the walls of some ruins and they hid as the three black helicopters came into view. As they came closer to the ground, Alice could see that most of the Biters had taken cover. Most, but not all. Two Biters were running around frantically, as if in a state of panic, trying to find safety. A door slid open in one of the helicopters and two men leaned out with sniper rifles at their shoulders. Two shots rang out and both Biters went down, their heads split open by high velocity rounds.

Alice looked around her at the Biters cowering behind the ruins and she saw them in a totally new light. She had grown up thinking of them as rabid, vicious creatures who had to be destroyed because their only reason for being was to destroy humans. Now as she looked at Bunny Ears and the others, she realized that they were absolutely terrified. They certainly did not display much by way of evolved intelligence, but they seemed more like a pack of terrified animals being hunted by humans than a band of evil, ferocious killers. She saw several of them shake in terror as the helicopters came closer to the ground.

She saw the golden trident and lightning bolt drawn on their side, and did not need to read the letters to know which group these represented. Zeus.

She had sometimes overheard her father talk about Private Military Contractors, and how much power they had begun to wield in the chaotic times before The Rising. She did not understand much of what had been talked among the adults, but knew that Zeus was the most powerful of those armies, and its power had only increased after The Rising and human governments had ceased to function. Nobody knew who really controlled them, but they were the only visibly organized, and certainly best armed, human army around. Every few months, they would visit the independent settlements like the one where Alice lived and try and ask for volunteers to join them, or try and coerce the settlements to accept the rule of the Central Committee. It was unknown who made up this Central Committee, but this group controlled Zeus and it was common knowledge in the Deadland, as the area where Alice lived had come to be known, that once you accepted their rule, you signed away your freedom.

Alice had been lucky to be born in a settlement that had been begun by her father and the remaining contingent of US Marines guarding the US Embassy in New Delhi. They had then linked up with a group of Indian Army officers and their families. So, unlike most other settlements in the Deadland that had proved easy prey both for human looters and Biters in the chaos that prevailed in the early days, their settlement had been able to repel the assaults, and quickly established a reputation of being a group not to be messed with easily. Even then, whenever the Zeus soldiers had come to visit, Alice had felt a stab of fear at their sight. The men she had grown up with were mostly professional soldiers, or men like her father, fighting to save their families. The Zeus troopers in contrast, were guns for hire, and displayed little compassion or sympathy for those in the Deadland. If you didn't join them, they would turn their back even when you were under assault by Biters.

As snipers on the helicopters provided cover, men

dressed all in black rappelled down from the helicopters and began fanning out. Alice was only too conscious of the reputation Zeus had, but right now between being herded to an unknown fate as a prisoner of the Biters, and getting a chance of going back home, even if it meant trusting the Zeus troopers, she would choose the latter in a heartbeat. She waited for the Zeus troopers to come closer, since she knew that if she tried to attract their attention too early, Bunny Ears and his friends would surely kill her. She kept waiting for the right moment, but then without her having to do anything, a distraction presented itself.

A female Biter near Alice lost her nerve and ran into the open, screeching wildly. Two Zeus troopers knelt and fired their weapons on full automatic at her, the criss-crossing lines of fire turning the Biter around like a puppet on a string, before she was thrown to the ground. When she tried to get up, a sniper on a helicopter shot her head off with a single bullet. Another Biter ran towards one of the doors leading to an underground base when several shots sent him down, and once again a sniper delivered the coup de grace.

Alice watched, realizing that this was no battle. This was a massacre. She saw Bunny Ears and the others with her huddling, as if deciding what to do, when she decided to make her move. She stepped out from behind cover, hoping that the Zeus troopers would not shoot her, and screamed at the top of her voice.

'Help me! I'm human!'

~ * * * ~

Alice's eyes widened in fear when instead of coming to her assistance one of the Zeus troopers knelt down and aimed his rifle at her. She was pushed to one side as the bullets tore through the air where she had stood scant seconds before. She looked up to see Bunny Ears glaring at her before he grabbed her by her arm and dragged her behind cover.

The Zeus troopers seemed to comprehend what was going on, and the fact that a young human girl seemed to be help captive by this horde of Biters galvanized them into action. More troopers rappelled out of the helicopters and they began advancing towards the wall behind which Alice was now hidden.

Bunny Ears whistled, an ear piercing sound that made Alice involuntarily cover her ears. When she peeked out the side of the wall, she saw what his signal had meant. All around the Zeus troopers, Biters gathered among the ruins and advanced upon them. The troopers opened fire and Alice saw several of the Biters fall, but the others were now advancing at speed. The snipers on the helicopters took out a few more Biters with carefully aimed head shots.

Alice looked on in fascination. She had directly participated in more than a dozen skirmishes with the Biters and witnessed a dozen or more as a spotter or during her training. At that time, it had been but natural to think of the Biters as the ferocious, formidable adversaries everyone said they were, and she had not even thought twice before emptying her clip into the undead Santa's head when he had blundered into their path during a patrol.

Now, sitting among the Biters and getting a glimpse of what battle against humans looked like from their perspective, she began to see things a bit differently. Sure, up close they were formidable, with their strength, seeming immunity to pain, and their single-minded dedication to biting human flesh. But in the open like this, against trained soldiers, they were cannon fodder. They could not use any weapons, moved slower than humans, and did not seem to have enough intelligence for anything more than the most rudimentary tactics.

The dozen or so Zeus soldiers were now tightly packed with their backs to each other, like a phalanx, and were moving steadily towards her position. They were still picking off targets at will, and dozens of Biters littered the ground around them. But the Biters kept coming, and Alice saw that at least two holes had opened up in the ground, and Biters were pouring through them, trying to get close enough to the soldiers to bring their teeth and nails to bear. It was a massacre, and Alice wondered what the Biters were trying to achieve by walking straight into certain annihilation, or were they just such mindless drones that they kept going, driven by instinct or bloodlust, regardless of the odds that faced them?

She felt a tug at her arm, and Bunny Ears pulled her up and dragged her along. She tried to resist, but his grip on her arm was so tight that she could not shake him off. When she kicked out at him, sending him staggering back, he nonchalantly slapped her across the face. The blow was so hard it knocked her down and she felt the ground spinning around her as Bunny Ears picked her up and slung her across his shoulders. He screeched loudly, and in apparent response, a dozen or more Biters stepped between them and the advancing Zeus troopers.

It became instantly clear to Alice that there was a method to what the Biters were doing. They were buying Bunny Ears some time so he could get her away. Why they wanted her so badly, and what the drawing on the wall had meant were beyond her, but what was certain was that her hopes of a rescue were being dashed. She could now see the Zeus troopers falter and start to withdraw in face of the sheer strength of numbers of the Biters. Before Bunny Ears ducked into some ruins, she saw the first Zeus trooper fall under a group of clawing and slashing Biters.

They were someplace dark, and Bunny Ears was

running through what appeared to be long corridors of some official building. There were doors lining the corridor, and Alice saw Biters hiding behind more than one of them. Even if any of the Zeus troopers got this far, in the confined and dark environment, they would be easy pickings for the hidden Biters. She began to reassess the Biters based on what she had just seen. Yes, they were clearly not as intelligent as humans, but they were displaying some sort of planning and forethought. But the big question still remained- what the hell did they want with her?

Bunny Ears ducked low under a collapsed beam and finally stopped, unceremoniously dumping Alice on the ground. She swore with the choicest of obscenities she had learnt from years spent in the company of soldiers and glared at him, but he just looked at her with no expression in his yellowing, vacant eyes. He pointed to a hole in the wall that he motioned for her to walk through. When she hesitated, he slapped her, sending her crashing to the ground again.

'What the hell is it with you? Stop hitting me and I may listen!'

Again, her words seemed to have no effect on Bunny Ears and so Alice, realizing she had no real options and no apparent means of escape, walked in through the hole, and began a steep descent underground. Just a few minutes ago, she had got her first glimpse of humans for the first time since she had been foolhardy enough to follow Bunny Ears down the hole, and had begun to entertain hopes of rescue. However, now she was again firmly in the clutches of the Biters, and headed back into one of their underground strongholds.

They walked for what seemed to be at least an hour in total darkness, and Bunny Ears finally stopped in an opening that was lit by a single torch. Alice grabbed her sides, with barely enough strength left to stay standing, let alone follow him any deeper.

'I need water, ok? I am not like you. I need to drink and eat.'

He looked at her, with no expression on his face, and she made drinking motions with her hands, hoping that he would get the idea. When he moved his right arm, Alice flinched, wondering if he would hit her again. Instead, he held out her backpack, which he had taken from her after the fight in the Embassy. She opened it and took out her water bottle, draining it as she drank every last drop there. When she put it back inside, she felt inside the bag for a second. She had her first aid kid, and one signal flare. While she had no weapons left on her, that flare might come in handy. When Bunny Ears growled, she handed the backpack to him, thankful that he was intelligent enough to understand what she wanted, but not quite smart enough to check the bag.

She followed him deeper into the abyss, going through several more descending turns before they arrived at a door. When Bunny Ears pushed it open, Alice saw that they had entered some sort of shelter that must have once been designed for use by humans. Metal bunk beds lined the room, in which dozens of Biters were sprawled. Some of them hissed and moved in her direction, but a series of growls from Bunny Ears sent them scampering back. Perhaps to keep her close and out of harm's way, he grabbed her wrist and pulled her behind him. Many of the Biters glared and spat at her, and she had no doubt they would have ripped her to shreds if her unlikely guardian in the form of a Biter with bunny ears had not been there.

They paused at an open door, and Alice froze when she heard a human voice coming from somewhere on the other side. It was a gravely voice, deep and slow, but it was unmistakably the voice of a human female, unless Alice was about to meet her first talking Biter.

'What have you brought down today? Let me see.'

Alice heard some growling and screeching in response, as the speaker continued.

'Two Zeus troopers? What on Earth would I want to do with them? Their papers show that they are but fresh recruits so they could have nothing of use for me. Of course, you would have no way of knowing that, would you?'

Alice heard more screeching, and listened to this surreal conversation, wondering if the two parties actually understood what they were saying to each other.

'Oh well, you have brought them down, and I did have a chat with them. Unfortunately, they are totally brainwashed and unwilling to join us and after what they've seen, I cannot let them go back up. I was hoping that they would have a more open mind. It's probably all for the better- these two are part of the unit that killed all the little ones a fortnight ago.'

The screeching now gave way to a blood-curdling roar, and Alice realized with a start that the Biter being talked to did understand what was being said to it. The next words from the female voice made Alice's eyes open wide with fear.

'Take them, and off with their heads.'

Alice heard the men begging and pleading as they were dragged away, and then Bunny Ears began to push her into the room. She pushed him back, now in a state of panic, wondering if she was being prepared for the same fate as had befallen the captured Zeus troopers.

'Let me go! Goddammit, let go of my hand!'

Suddenly she heard the female voice inside the room call out to her in a soothing tone.

'It's quite all right, dear. I suspect you have nothing to fear from me. Come on in.'

'Who the hell are you?'

The voice tut-tutted, like a disapproving school

teacher.

'Young lady, I had hoped for better manners from someone from one of the settlements. You are not one of the wild humans roaming and scavenging in the Deadland. Come on in, and we can talk like civilized people. As for who I am, these fellows down here think I'm their Queen.'

And so, shivering with fear, Alice was pushed into the room for her audience with the Queen of the Biters.

THREE

WHEN ALICE ENTERED THE ROOM, she found herself in what resembled an office of some sort, with a large couch at one end, and a desk with a high-backed chair at the other. The Queen was sitting in the chair, but had her back turned to the door, so Alice could see little more of her than a gloved arm resting on the chair's side. Bunny Ears was standing behind her, and making vaguely threatening growling noises. Alice had no idea how they communicated, but she thought a fair attempt at translation would indicate that he was reminding her not to try anything since he was right behind her. That suited Alice just fine, since she was so terrified that any act of bravado was the last thing on her mind.

'Dear, please sit down, and don't mind Rabbit there. He's just very protective but is otherwise quite gentle.'

Alice found it impossible to contain a dismissive snort as she considered how anyone could think of a vicious Biter as gentle. The Queen seemed not to notice, or at any rate, take any offense, and so Alice sat down on the couch and waited. When the chair swiveled around, Alice's curiosity was in overdrive and she was leaning so far forward that she was on the verge of falling off the couch. Then she got her first glimpse of the Queen, and to say that she was let down would be quite the understatement of the century.

The Queen of the Biters looked like a friendly librarian at the local library, complete with her grey hair tied in a neat bun, and dark tinted glasses perched on the edge of her nose, framing an aging, tired, but kind face. Of course, Alice had never been to a library, and had never seen a librarian, but the figure she saw in front of her was the farthest thing possible from the fearsome Biter leader she had half-expected to see. As the Queen got up, Alice saw that she was most certainly not a Biter, with her face unblemished, and that she was evidently Indian, for she wore a saree that hung loosely around her thin frame.

'Are you the Queen?'

The old lady smiled, as she came closer to Alice.

'My name was Protima, though nobody has called me by that name in a very long time. In our world, I guess I am considered the Queen, though what I rule over is something I myself am not very sure of. Now, young lady, let me take a look at you and see if what has got these fellows so excited has any basis in fact or not.'

When the Queen came closer and took off her glasses, Alice gasped and shrank back.

The Queen's face may have looked as unblemished as that of any healthy human, but her eyes were red, dilated and lifeless, the eyes of the undead. When she grinned, Alice saw crusted blood on her lips and around the corners of her mouth. Alice began to scream, but a gloved hand was clamped over her mouth.

'Shh, dear. There's nothing to be so terrified of. Yet.'

With that, the Queen grabbed a lock of Alice's hair and pulled on it hard enough to make Alice grimace.

'Well, it is real blond hair. When these fools came in blabbering about a blond haired Alice, I was sure they had got it wrong. Who would have expected a young blond girl in the middle of what was once Delhi?'

Alice was sitting frozen in place. Somehow, the combination of her unblemished face and her ability to speak so articulately made the Queen even more fearsome than the most outwardly bloodthirsty and fearsome Biters Alice had ever encountered. Finally, she mustered up the courage to speak.

'Are you one of...'

She never got a chance to complete her question as the Queen snapped back.

'One of the undead? One of the Biters? What other hateful label were you planning to use? That's always been the problem with humans. You take anything you fear and cannot understand and make it an object of hate. So much easier to hate and destroy than to seek to understand.'

Actually, Alice had been about to just say 'them', but she was too scared to interrupt the Queen's rant, so she just sat in silence and waited for what was to come next. The Queen sat down next to Alice and took off her gloves. Alice saw that underneath the gloves were not the hands of a healthy human, but yellowed, decayed and blood crusted hands criss-crossed with open wounds and bite marks. When the Queen laid a cold, hard hand on Alice's wrist, she involuntarily flinched, but the vice like grip on her wrist prevented her from moving. In a brief moment of panic, Alice contemplated striking out, but a low growl behind her warned her that Bunny Ears was right there, watching her every move.

'Dear, you must be wondering what all the fuss is about, right?'

Alice noticed that the Queen's face was twitching and while her lifeless eyes betrayed no emotion, she seemed excited like a little girl at a toy shop.

'It is the prophecy I had made. It is finally coming true, and that means that our days of suffering will come to an end.'

Alice had no idea what the Queen was talking about, so she just waited for her to continue.

'Don't you see? You must be the one the book told me about.'

'What book?'

The Queen got up, and Alice saw that she was virtually hopping in excitement. At that point, Alice realized that human or undead, one thing was for sure. The Queen was totally unhinged. The Queen walked back to her desk and fished in the drawers for a few seconds before bringing out something covered in a coarse cloth. As soon as she raised the package in her hands, Alice saw that Bunny Ears had gone down on his knees. Several thoughts were buzzing through her mind. Since when did mindless Biters get religious? How the hell was this so-called Queen partly human and partly Biter? How was it at all possible that she of all people had anything to do with any prophecy this crazed old Queen claimed to have made?

The Queen was now in front of Alice and holding the package in front of her.

'Do you realize what this is?'

Of course Alice had no way of knowing, but she was young enough to not know a rhetorical question, so she shook her head. Any response on her part was largely unnecessary because the Queen was in a trance like state, talking without a pause.

'When the mad human governments rained fire, I hid in the underground chambers that they had made as bomb shelters and old sewers, moving from one tunnel to another. Do you know how long I was down there?'

30

Another rhetorical question, and then the Queen continued.

'I kept my phone running as long as I could, turning it on for a few seconds every day to see the time and date. When I lost it, it had been three months. I had been bitten seven times.'

The Queen put the package on the sofa next to Alice and raised her sleeves, showing a bloody, mangled mess on her hands. Alice wondered again how this woman had retained some human faculties despite so obviously having been bitten by Biters. Also, she shuddered to think just how horrible it must have been to wander alone in the dark tunnels, surrounded by crazed Biters in utter darkness, with no easy access to food or water. Anybody would have lost their mind in such circumstances. The Queen continued.

'I would have given up and killed myself if I had been just a human, but as you can see, I was becoming something more. I did not have much to eat, so I scrounged around for herbs and leaves. And one day, I found this.'

She motioned to the package.

'At the time, I didn't know what to make of it, but when I came back to the surface and saw what the world had been reduced to, I realized it was perhaps the last book left in the Deadland.'

The Queen took a break and went back to her desk, bringing out a bunch of green leaves that she proceeded to chew raw. Alice could hear Bunny Ears growling in anticipation and the Queen threw him a couple of leaves that he gobbled down. Alice recognized the leaves as ganja leaves and remembered the warnings from the adults about never eating them. If this woman, or Biter, or whatever the Queen was, had been living on ganja leaves for months, no wonder her mind was a bit messed up with all the hallucinations it must have caused. That feeling was cemented in her mind when the Queen took out what was in the package and held it before Alice.

'Behold the prophecy I was given by the last book left in the Deadland. A vision of you coming to lead us to victory.'

Alice saw what the Queen was holding and saw a slightly charred book cover. It showed a blonde girl jumping into a hole after a rabbit, and Alice suddenly realized that it must have inspired the drawing she had seen and also explained why they had been so excited to see her. She could not immediately make out all the words, but saw her name on top. The Queen seemed a bit disappointed at the lack of recognition from Alice, but then she did not know that Alice had not read a single book in her life, and did not recognize the title on the cover.

Alice in Wonderland.

~ * * * ~

There must have been hundreds, if not more Biters crowding the large underground hall in front of the Queen, all down on their knees. They kept up a constant crescendo of howling and screeching that made Alice want to put her hands over her ears. But her hands were pinned behind her by Bunny Ears and the Queen was now addressing her troops.

'Look at her! The prophecy is true! She will lead us to victory and we will throw off the oppression and savagery of those evil humans forever. They did not want to coexist with us but now we will have a chance to make them understand, to accept us, and let us survive side by side with men. Otherwise, we will wage our final war for survival and make them understand that we can and will become the dominant species on this planet.'

The Biters seemed incapable of speaking in any human tongue but they seemed to understand the Queen just fine, and soon they had worked themselves into a frenzy. The more Alice saw them, the more they resembled wild animals, and the Queen ended her exhortation by asking them to prepare for their missions that night.

Alice was herded back to the small room that was effectively her cell. She had no idea of how the Queen expected her to lead her forces to victory. What could one young girl contribute? Moreover, Alice had no intention whatsoever of playing out whatever role the Queen had imagined for her in her delusional prophecy. She was just biding her time, waiting for when she could escape, and so, for now she decided that playing along with the Queen was her best strategy. Her chance came sooner than she had expected when later that evening the Queen sent for her.

'Alice, they look to me to be their leader, but I was an old woman even before I transformed, and while I had my skills, being able to fight and lead in battle was not one of them. You are the one who must take on my mantle and continue our struggle.'

Alice could take it no longer and blurted out.

'What struggle? Why don't you just leave humans alone? What harm have we done to you that you lead these creatures to attack us?'

The Queen sat down, and while a smile played at he edges of her lips, her eyes were as lifeless as ever.

'I don't blame you for believing what you do. You've grown up hearing only one side of the story, and from my old life I know just how good the powers that be are at propaganda.'

She saw the skeptical look on Alice's face and continued.

'I won't try and convince you because my words would be of no value to you. So I will let you see through your own eyes.'

She nodded and Bunny Ears grabbed Alice by her arm and led her out. She was dragged more than led up a series of winding tunnels and then suddenly she found herself outside again. It was getting dark outside and she was in a thickly wooded area. She saw a broken sign and she recognized the symbols from some of her training when they had been familiarized with the surrounding landscape. They were near the Yamuna River, or rather what used to be the river, but now was a dried up trickle after the nuclear firestorms and subsequent battles had destroyed the dams and reservoirs feeding it. She sensed movement around her and she saw that there were at least a dozen more Biters hiding among the trees.

After more than an hour of waiting, she turned to Bunny Ears, asking him what it was he had brought her here to see, but he merely grunted in reply, as if telling her to shut up and wait. Then as she watched, something strange happened. She saw a large group of Biters emerge from the trees, perhaps a hundred or more of them. They were all walking in single file, which was totally contrary to the image Alice had grown up with of them being savage, mindless brutes incapable of any act of co-ordination or reason. But what totally took her breath away was the fact that the Biters were not just a random group out to inflict violence, but seemed to be a social grouping of some sort. There were a handful of women, many of them carrying small children. The children themselves looked like something out of a nightmare, with their yellowed skin, and many cuts and bruises on their blood covered bodies, but all the same, they were children. Alice had no idea if these were families formed and born after the adults had been transformed to Biters of if these were families that had retained some of their old bonds even after they ceased to be human. Either way, yet again irrevocable proof was in front of her eyes that there was much more to the Biters than she had been brought up to believe.

As the column came closer, Alice got a better look

at them. With their bowed backs and trundling along slowly in single file, they looked more like a group of refugees than a band of marauding monsters. She heard Bunny Ears screech behind her, and two Biters in the group ahead responded in kind. What was the Queen trying to show her by sending her here? True, there seemed to be much more to the Biters than what she had grown up believing, but so far she had seen nothing that would change her mind about joining the Queen or fulfilling some deranged prophecy of hers. No, if there was one thing Alice was sure of, it was the fact that she would find the earliest possible opportunity to escape.

Just then, the convoy in front of her stopped in its tracks, many of the adults looking up at the skies. Several of children began howling, their inhuman cries making Alice's hair stand up on end. She didn't know what had suddenly brought about the change in their behavior, but within a few seconds, the group transformed from an orderly convoy to a totally panic-stricken mob. The Biters were now screaming and running in such a panic that she saw more than one run into trees and fall down. Bunny Ears had now emerged and was howling, an ear-splitting noise that was taken up by the others who had been hiding in the trees with him. It almost looked like he and the others had been sent by the Queen to shepherd the group to safety through the woods, but now there was no more semblance of order. The Biters were running around screaming like wild animals that have caught a scent of hunters and one of them, a woman with a bloodied and mangled child in her arms, came within a few feet of Alice. She glared at Alice with hate-filled eyes, and baring bloodied teeth, seemed ready to pounce when Bunny Ears knocked her off her feet with a blow to the back of her head.

Alice still didn't know what had caused such bedlam when she heard a familiar sound. The whirring rotors of approaching helicopters. She looked up to see several black helicopters approach the clearing. Zeus had arrived.

~ * * * ~

The female Biter who had been knocked over by Bunny Ears was getting up unsteadily on one knee when her head exploded in a spray of blood. Alice screamed and dove for cover behind a tree as more snipers aboard the oncoming helicopters opened fire. She watch three more Biters caught in the open fall, their heads split open by high-powered sniper rifles, before the others scattered among the trees. The child the Biter had been carrying was now feet away from Alice, and looking at its hideous form, with its mangled face and bloody skin, it was hard to feel any emotion the way one felt towards human children. Alice was about to crawl away under the bushes nearby and try and escape, but something held her back. She looked back at the child again, and this time his eyes met hers. There was no innocence, no love, just the blank, hate-filled expression that was characteristic of Biters and while he could not even walk, he began to crawl towards her, baring a handful of half-formed teeth. The rational part of Alice's mind told her to run, but she was transfixed at the sight of this little child who would no doubt bite Alice and transform her into a Biter like him given half a chance, yet who was little more than a child. A helpless child.

Just then, a huge Biter easily standing more than six and a half feet tall ran over in front of her. He was wearing a floppy hat and much of the left side of his face was missing. He picked up the child and ran towards the nearby trees as Alice heard a fresh burst of firing. This time it was not the distinctive pops of sniper rifles, but the staccato bursts of automatic weapon fire. That could mean only one thing- Zeus troopers were now on the ground.

Alice looked to her left and saw something was which no less than a miracle- her backpack, which Bunny Ears must have dropped there in the chaos. She remembered the signal flare that had been there and crawled towards the backpack, grabbing it before she again retreated behind cover. She unzipped it, and breathed a sigh of relief as she saw the signal flare was still there. She looked around and saw that Bunny Ears was nowhere to be seen. Now was her chance. She popped the flare and soon a red light shot up in the sky. She watched it sail above the treeline and hoped that it would get the attention of the Zeus troopers and someone would come to get her.

She did succeed in attracting attention all right, but of entirely the unwanted variety when she saw two Biters homing in on her. They were screaming and coming at her with their teeth bared. Alice realized with a shudder that one of them must have claimed a victim in the fighting now going on all around her since his mouth was covered with fresh blood that was dripping onto his muddy and torn shirt. There was no time and no place to run, so Alice got ready to face her attackers. The first to reach her was the man with the bloody face, a thin man who was missing his left arm below the elbow and seemed to have half his hair burnt off. As he screamed and leapt towards Alice, she went down on a knee, sweeping him off his feet. She had no weapons with her, but she brought her foot down on the biter's windpipe in a crushing kick. It would have killed a grown man, but the Biter screamed and began to get up again. The second Biter, a tall man wearing a blood stained vest and shorts was now almost upon her. Alice ran towards him dodging his outstretched arms and then turned around on her heels to kick his foot from under him behind his knee. It shattered his leg, but as Alice well knew, that would hardly be enough to stop a Biter on the rampage. He got up unsteadily on one leg, as Alice tried to run only to come straight in the path of the first Biter, whose neck now hung at an awkward angle, but his mouth was open and he lunged at her.

Alice closed her eyes, bracing herself for the attack that never came. She heard a loud pop and when she opened her eyes she saw the Biter's headless body lying just a couple of feet from her. The second Biter, now limping towards her met a similar fate as another round slammed into his head.

She looked into the trees ahead and saw a black clad man kneeling, a rifle at his shoulder. He wore the black battle dress of the Zeus troopers, but unlike the others she had seen, he had no helmet to cover his close-cropped black hair, which was covered with flecks of grey. He saw her and grinned and began to run towards her.

Alice took a step towards him, her heart racing in anticipation of her coming rescue when three Biters jumped out of the trees and in the path of the Zeus trooper who was less than a hundred meters from her. He shot one in the head at point blank range before another Biter knocked the rifle out of his hand. Alice had been trained to fight since she was a child, but she had never seen anyone fight like the Zeus trooper in front of her. Unfazed by the loss of his gun, he unsheathed a large knife at his belt and jumped up, bringing it down into the skull of the nearest Biter, who screamed and went down, not to get down again. The third Biter was now almost upon him, and he rolled out of the way, taking out his handgun and put three shots into the Biter's head.

Two more Zeus troopers now appeared, and judging by their salutes and the deference they showed the grey haired man, it seemed that he was an officer of some sort. He pointed to her and the two of them began to jog towards her. That was when the large Biter with the hat came crashing out of the trees.

He grabbed the nearest trooper and snapped his neck, the sickening crunching sound carrying to Alice. The second trooper tried to bring his rifle to bear, but the Biter bit him on the neck, and he went down spurting blood. Alice knew what would come next. The trooper spasmed and went rigid, and when he got up again, Alice saw that his eyes were the vacant, lifeless eyes of the undead. His head exploded as the grey haired officer fired, preferring to kill his own man versus having him turn into one of the undead, as the Biter with the hat reared up to his full height and screamed. More than a dozen Biters now emerged into the clearing and the Zeus officer retreated into the trees, looking at Alice once. As their eyes met, he cocked his arm back and threw something at her before he disappeared into the trees, pursued by the Biters.

The object he had thrown landed a couple of feet away from Alice, and she ran to pick up what he had thrown just as Bunny Ears reappeared with three other Biters. He grabbed her arm to pull her away but before he yanked her away, she looked at the small blinking object in her hand. It was a radio beacon that would give away her position as long as she carried it. There was to be no escape today, but as she slipped the beacon into her pockets, she felt a new surge of hope.

Help would be on the way soon.

~ * * * ~

'So, what did you learn from your trip?'

The question had been asked as if the Queen were enquiring about a field trip to a museum instead of her having just been in the middle of a life and death struggle, so Alice wasn't quite sure what the Queen had in mind. That became clear when the giant Biter with the hat appeared and uttered a series of guttural growls.

'Hatter here tells me that you caused a fair bit of inconvenience, but if anything is to be learnt from today's experience, do learn that we are not fools. We did not send you out to offer you an easy and convenient escape route.'

'So why did you send me out there? I've seen enough battles and there's nothing I saw that I haven't seen before.'

The Queen turned on Alice with a fury, baring her teeth, and for a second Alice was truly fearful that she would attack her, but then the Queen seemed to control herself with a conscious effort of will and answered in a soft voice.

'You just used your usual prejudices to filter out what you didn't want to see. I wanted you to see us as we are- a society, a group of sentient beings. Different from humans, but no less deserving of the right to exist. Not animals to be hunted down and exterminated.'

That did ring a bell with Alice. True, she had never imagined that Biters could be organized in some sort of social unit, and certainly had never bargained for the fact that she would see babies and what appeared to be their parents together. Still, that did not change the fundamental equation. The anger at all the cruelty she had seen Biters visit upon humans in her life came back to her as she answered the Queen with a bitter tinge in her voice.

'I have seen enough innocent humans slaughtered by Biters. I have seen babies bitten by Biters. I have seen good, decent people turn into bloodthirsty Biters after being bitten. So it's not as if your precious Biters are innocent, helpless victims.'

The Queen hissed, though Alice sensed more regret than rage in her reaction.

'I had hoped you would begin to change your mind and embrace your destiny, but it looks like your mind is still too closed. Oh well, I hope you can reflect on it over the next few days.'

With that, the giant Biter referred to as Hatter gripped her arm and pushed her roughly out of the room. She was led to a small, dark room and the door slammed shut once she went in. Alice huddled alone in a corner of the cold, dark room, and took out the beacon from her pocket. She watched the small blinking red light till exhaustion overtook her and she fell into an uneasy slumber. She dreamt of a Biter baby having its head shot off, and she woke up covered in sweat. There was no more sleep to be had that night.

FOUR

IF THE QUEEN'S INTENT HAD been to torture Alice into submission, Alice thought she was doing a pretty good job of it. For the next two days, she got nothing to eat or drink other than a single glass of dirty water that was shoved into her room once a day. The room was totally dark all the time and Alice soon lost track of time. She screamed her rage out for the first few hours but then just sat in silence against the wall. She may have been trained as a warrior from an early age, but nobody had ever trained her on what to do if she were captured. It had never occurred to anyone that someone could be taken prisoner by the Biters.

Finally, hungry, thirsty and disoriented, she was on the verge of asking for the Queen and agreeing to whatever crazy prophecy she seemed to believe in. Anything to get out of the room, anything to get a bite to eat or a drink of clean water. That was when Bunny Ears opened the door and pulled her out, leading her to the Queen's room. Alice found the Queen sitting at her desk, chewing ganja leaves and holding the charred book that seemed so important to her. When Alice entered the room, she called out loudly for food, and Hatter came in, holding a hunk of nearly stale bread. As disgusting as it looked, it was the first food Alice had seen in almost three days and she hungrily wolfed it down.

The Queen waited for her to finish and then sat down in front of Alice, the book on her lap.

'Alice, I was wrong. In my anger, I thought that frightening and intimidating you would bring you to my side, but if you are to fulfill the prophecy, it cannot be through fear. It has to be because you believe in our cause.'

Alice, bitter and angry after what she had endured over the last two days, blurted out.

'Yeah, and locking me in a dark room and starving me will make me believe in your prophecy? Or will it be the bloody ganja leaves you gulp down?'

Alice saw the muscles on the Queen's face tighten and once again she saw a glimpse of the rage she was capable of, but she controlled herself as she responded to Alice.

'No, you remember the old quote about the truth setting us free.'

Alice had never heard the quote, but listened as the Queen continued.

'Tell me, what do you know about what you humans call The Rising?'

Growing up, Alice had heard the story many times from her parents, and then it had been amplified and embellished by countless conversations with other kids, so the answer to her was obvious.

'Everyone knows about it. One day, something happened, and the dead started coming to life. Before anyone could do anything, they started attacking others, and those bitten turned into...Biters, I guess. They couldn't be killed other than through a shot through the head, and they soon overran most cities. Then the governments got desperate and bombed the cities after evacuating as many people as possible....'

She couldn't complete because the Queen had got up and screamed, an inhuman howl that shocked Alice so much that she got up from her chair, which clattered to the ground behind her. The Queen was now speaking fast and with such anger that spittle was flying from her mouth.

'It did not just happen. We made it happen.'

Alice wasn't sure what she was referring to and asked what she meant.

'Us. Human governments or at least some elements in our governments. The US government had been experimenting with chemical and biological agents that would transform our troops into super-soldiers, into beserkers immune to pain. At the same time, there was research on modifying these to create agents that would drive enemy troops insane, a rage virus which would transform them into wild animals who would kill each other. We experimented with rats, with monkeys and.....with humans.'

Alice found that hard to believe and gasped aloud.

'No, dear. We did all that. In secret facilities in Afghanistan and other places. We were drunk with our power, imagining what would happen if we could drop one single canister of this agent in the middle of an enemy army division. It would tear itself to pieces without us firing a shot. Then it all came apart.'

'What happened?'

'The Chinese found out what we were up to, and they knew that if we perfected this, we would be invincible. They infiltrated our program, and destroyed our key research lab in the US. We couldn't prove anything- it looked like an explosion caused by a gas cylinder, but we knew who was behind it. The American economy was in deep recession, China was on the ascendant, and this was our last hope in keeping them in check. We had extra stores of the agent the Chinese did not know about, and we decided to teach them a lesson, to show them that we were still the superpower. A covert mission was authorized and we dropped the agent into a village in Mongolia. It was the first time it had been used on humans outside controlled conditions, and nobody knew what to expect. I had pleaded against the decision, so many of us had, but we were overruled. Thousands fell, then tens of thousands as it spread.'

Alice knew only vaguely of the politics between countries of the Old Days, since national boundaries and the old countries now hardly mattered, but she found it hard to believe that people could have done this to themselves.

'What happened then? If you were in America then how did it spread there?'

The Queen sat down again.

'Hundreds of people were injured in the blast at the lab and were exposed to all the toxins and agents we were working on. The next day, they started transforming and biting all those around them.'

A chill went up Alice's spine, yet her mind refused to believe what she was hearing.

'Why should I believe you?'

The Queen went to her desk and fished out an identification card and some papers. Alice struggled to read what was on them, but the emblem of what she knew to be the United States Government was there.

'I was one of the head researchers on this project. I was born here in India but did my Doctorate in the US and joined the Department of Defense. I thought it was exciting, to be able to come up with new ways of treating our wounded, to make the world safer, but then we all got a bit drunk with our own power, and we started meddling with things we should have left alone. We tried to play God, and we were not ready for what we unleashed. When the decision to attack China was made, I quit and came back to India, but by then, nowhere was safe any more. At first, after being bitten, people changed after a few hours, so you had many cases of people being attacked in airport terminals and boarding their flights after what they thought were minor cuts. In days, all air travel was banned, but when you have tens of millions traveling by air every day, it spread like wildfire.'

Alice still refused to believe what she was hearing, so it was only harder for her to believe what came next.

'And the Great Fires, that too was of our making, of our petty jockeying for power. It began with the US and China using tactical nukes on each other. It had nothing to do with making the world secure from the so-called Biters. It was man destroying the world when it looked like all that mattered to us then- power, money, oil, were now going to be worthless. It was as if all the old rules and taboos were broken. Then Pakistan joined the party, and India retaliated. Iran and Israel nuked it out. Between the attacks and the spreading of the virus, the world became what it is, and nobody bothered to do the one thing that could have stopped it all.'

'And what was that?'

The Queen looked straight at Alice.

'We had a vaccine, Alice. We could have cured them all if we had chosen to co-operate and not turn on each other.'

~ * * * ~

Alice barely slept that night, despite being placed in a much more comfortable room with a mattress and a table with clean water on it. She didn't want to believe the Queen, she didn't want to believe that humans could have been so savage. All her life, the Biters had been the boogeymen, the monsters of our nightmares that had emerged from the dead to turn on humans. Her mind found it impossible to process the possibility that humans had been responsible for starting it all.

Unable to contain her curiosity, she went back to the Queen's chambers and found her sitting on her chair, reading the charred book that she held so dear. Did Biters never sleep? She looked up as Alice walked in.

'So Alice, as the story in this fine book goes, have you become curiouser and curiouser?'

Alice had no idea what she was talking about so she got to the point.

'You have no proof for anything you've said. Maybe you did work in the Government, but everything else could be a story. I don't know why you think I have anything to do with this, or why your finding that book makes it a prophecy, but there's no reason for me to believe you.'

The Queen got up and went to her desk and brought out a small vial with a red cap that had a syringe in it. She held out the vial in front of Alice.

'Here is the vaccine. The last and only dose I know of. When the outbreak started, one of my colleagues in the US sent me a couple of vaccines. The Government had limited stocks and was starting to vaccinate key leaders, so it was a really big deal for her to try and save me.'

'If there is a vaccine, why didn't they save others?'

The Queen stopped, looking at the vial.

'Good question. Many of us believed that they did not want to.'

'Why would they do that?'

'There were always rumors, but nothing more than rumors about how some powerful groups were actively manipulating events to create a New World Order. They believed the world was getting overpopulated and wanted to start over, with a select group of elites in charge. Powerful people, in Government, in the Military, in Banks engineering all this behind the scenes. The times before The Rising were one of chaos-many economies were in deep decline, and common people were starting to rise against the elite who seemed to get richer even as common folks lost their jobs and got poorer. The rumors said that these elites were seeing their grasp on power slip away and so they had a long-term plan to wipe out much of the population and start afresh. That's where people like Zeus come in- they could not rely on the Military to do all their dirty work, and that's why in the last few years before The Rising, Private Military Contractors were getting so prominent and powerful.'

For Alice, this was all too incredible to believe. Secret private armies, human elites trying to re-engineer the world and so on. What she had grown up knowing was so much simpler, and it was tempting to believe the simpler version than even consider such a possibility.

'If that was their plan, they succeeded, right?'

The Queen looked and Alice saw the hint of a smile on the corners of her lips.

'We came in the way. They had never bargained for just how.....contagious this turned out to be, or indeed the fact that so many of us survived by going underground into sewers and bomb shelters. They thought we would be mindless animals who would wander around and get nuked, but I led so many of us underground and then we emerged.'

Alice now asked the question that had been on her mind from the beginning.

'Excuse me, but what happened to you?'

'As things unraveled, and I found out more about the possible conspiracy · behind all this, I got very disillusioned and angry and started reaching out to people. One of my sources told me that there were elites in the Unites States who were colluding with elements in the Chinese government to orchestrate all this. They tried to kill me twice with the Zeus thugs and I went into hiding. But when the chaos took Delhi, I was attacked and bitten. I had two doses of the vaccine on me, and I injected myself seconds after being bitten. I was unconscious for several hours and I woke up the way I am. I don't understand it entirely but perhaps the combination of being bitten and than taking the vaccine within seconds left me this way. Many aspects of me were transformed, but I could still think like a human, and I was furious at what we had done to ourselves, and what we had allowed to happen.'

'What about the other Bit...'

'I saw them for who they really are. Yes, they are very unlike the people they were as humans. What the virus does, especially as it mutates over time, is activate the most primitive parts of the brain- so you get no sensation of pain, hyper aggressiveness and an almost reflexive desire to reproduce- in this case, bite others to increase their numbers.'

Alice refused to think of the Biters as just innocent victims.

'Wait a minute, I have seen so many innocent settlements and groups massacred by the Biters. They aren't just scared innocent animals.'

The Queen sighed, a gesture that made her suddenly seem much more human.

'We are all animals. We all experience fear, and when scared, we lash out. That's what you and the other human survivors have been doing. I can't make them understand everything I know since their brains have regressed a lot, but they are in awe of me because I am like them yet I can speak and can think more rationally- I helped save thousands of them by bringing them into these underground shelters.'

'What about this prophecy of yours?'

The Queen now had the book in her hands again.

'Oh that is very real. I found the book when I had lost all hope, and in that fevered dream, I saw you. I saw us finally reclaiming the world from the evil men who made this happen. I saw us and humans stop fighting each other.'

'It was just a dream.'

'Every prophecy is a dream, but if we believe in something, we can make it happen. The powers behind this conspiracy have a vested interest in keeping this war alive. Have you considered how they keep those helicopters flying? How do they get those weapons, and why do they focus so much on brining more and more human settlements under their control using the fear of Biters as an excuse? We fight it out in these barren wastelands while the elites behind all of this are perhaps living in luxury somewhere, in their own settlements from which they rule over us, with all the wealth and resources of the world at their disposal. You've seen only the Zeus troopers since they patrol the Deadland, but I know they are commanded by Red Guards, Chinese shock troops. I have seen them myself near Zeus bases beyond the Deadland. How is it the Chinese still seem to have such an organized force?'

Suddenly a beeping noise came from Alice's pockets and she froze in fear. She had forgotten all about the beacon. The Queen reached out and took out the small sphere from Alice's pocket and recoiled as she saw the logo on the side.

'What have you done?'

Then Alice started hearing the dull thud of explosions overhead.

~ * * * ~

Alice used the distraction of the explosions to bolt from the room, narrowly evading Bunny Ears' outstretched arms. The Queen was screaming now, all human speech and civility replaced by the wild screeching of Biters. Alice heard footsteps behind her, and given the rage the Queen had flown into, Alice thought it more prudent to get to safety instead of trying to reason with her. The sound of explosions was now closer and Alice ran into a corridor that seemed to lead towards the explosions. Overwhelmed by panic and the hope that she might get back to her parents, Alice put aside all that the Queen had said and focused on finding whoever had come to rescue her.

She came across a group of four Biters huddled in a corner and realized just how foolhardy she had been in running out alone. Without the Queen or Bunny Ears to save her, and with the attack on the base unfolding outside, the Biters would tear her to shreds. The four of them took one look at Alice and stood, moving towards her with their teeth bared. In such a confined space, the only silver lining was that they would have to come for her one by one, and she used that to her advantage. As the first Biter, a fat woman with her scalp half shorn off came within reach, Alice kicked her in the chest, putting all her body weight behind the kick. The kick sent the Biter stumbling back and into the path of the one behind her, and the two of them stumbled down in an ungainly heap. However, Alice had lost her footing and was now on the floor. She knew she was now in severe danger. There was no way she could fight off all four Biters in such a confined space, and with Bunny Ears and others likely chasing her, there was no question of her going back the way she had come.

As the first Biter reached for Alice, his head exploded and he fell to the side. The other Biters turned to face this new threat and within seconds, all three were down, with their heads split open by precisely aimed shots. Alice looked down the passageway to see three black-clad soldiers. She recognized one of them as the grey-haired officer she had seen in the forest. He waved at her with his assault rifle.

'Come over here!'

As she ran towards them, she heard howling

behind her. The officer shouted to his two men.

'Set up Claymores here and let's withdraw.'

Both troopers set the anti-personnel mines and then joined Alice and the officer who were already racing up the tunnel. Alice saw some movement to her right and dove to the ground just as a Biter hiding in an opening jumped at them. The trooper behind her was not so lucky as the big Biter grabbed him and bit his throat. The trooper's screams soon gave way to gurgling pleas for help as he fell to the ground, bleeding from his throat and face. The grey-haired officer with her kicked the Biter off his comrade and then shot him in the head twice. He then paused and looked at the fallen soldier, and Alice saw him close his eyes as he shot him in the head.

They then continued running up the tunnel. Alice could now see the light ahead from the tunnel's opening as they heard the Claymore mines explode behind them. As they got closer to the opening, she saw more than a dozen Zeus troopers, each carrying an assault rifle and standing at attention. The officer shouted to them.

'Hold them while I call in the air strike! The Red Guard jet should be on patrol now.'

Alice stumbled out, slipping and falling on the grass outside which was slick with the dew that came with Delhi winter nights as the troopers took position and began firing into the tunnel. The officer pulled her to one side and asked her to wait while he reached into a backpack lying nearby for a handheld radio.

'Apache One requests immediate air strike at last reported co-ordinates. We'll be clear in five.'

With that, he ordered his men to plant a few more mines at the entrance and then get as far away from the tunnel as possible. It seemed like an eternity since Alice had been standing in front of the Queen, but in reality it had all taken less than five minutes. Alice was still in a bit of shock, and followed meekly when the officer pulled her along. It was now nearly Sunset and the sky was beginning to darken as they jogged to a nearby hill and then the officer pushed her down, telling her to lie flat. She saw the other troopers take up position next to them. She now had a clear look at the tunnel, from which Biters were flowing out. The troopers all had their rifles at their shoulders and were firing away. Many of the Biters were hit by bursts of full automatic fire and twisted and turned before falling. Alice knew only a head shot would take them out permanently, but the damage the bullets did would make sure many of them never walked, as she saw legs torn off by the land mines and withering fire. She had accurately read the officer's mind as he bellowed to his men.

'Don't bother with head shots. Take their legs off so they can't move away from the target zone in time.'

Suddenly Alice saw the entire tunnel disappear behind a giant cloud of smoke and a split second later she heard the deafening boom of the explosion. The shock wave almost lifted her off the ground and as she looked again, she saw that the tunnel had largely caved in and there was a gaping hole in the ground, exposing the warren of tunnels underneath. There were dozens of Biters littered around, their bodies burning in the wreckage.

The officer spoke calmly into his radio.

'One more pass. Aim for the opening.'

Alice heard the roar of an aircraft flying overhead and looked up to see a dark shape silhouetted against the setting Sun. It turned towards them and dove down, and Alice saw a small cylinder detach itself from the aircraft and track down towards the tunnel. It entered the hole opened by the previous explosion, and once again there was a thunderous explosion as the bomb struck home. Alice had never witnessed such an awesome demonstration of firepower and she was in total awe of what Zeus seemed to be capable of when the officer told her to keep going.

'Some of the critters must have got out and will be around among the trees. So we can't afford to wait.'

They ran through the forest, and Alice was soon setting the pace that the Zeus troopers were trying hard to match up to. When the officer yelled for her to stop in a clearing, she saw that he was panting a bit when he caught up with her.

'You sure are fast. Wait here while I radio in to confirm where our pickup zone is.'

The troopers set up a perimeter as the officer radioed in. It was now nearly pitch black and Alice was beginning to get worried. It was one thing to bomb the Biters from thousands of feet in the air as the Zeus forces or these so called Red Guards had done, but it was quite another to contend with them on the ground in the dark. Alice had grown up in an environment where knowing how to best survive exactly in such circumstances was the difference between life and death every single day. As she scanned the Zeus troopers around her in the dim light thrown up by their emergency lights, she realized that for all their heavy weaponry and fancy equipment, they looked terrified. Only the officer seemed a bit composed, and as he finished asking for the helicopters to zero in on their lights, he smiled at her.

'I never introduced myself. My name is Colonel Dewan and I am in charge of the North Indian operations for Zeus.'

'Hi, I'm Alice Gladwell.'

Dewan smiled as he packed his radio.

'Alice, everyone knows who you are by now. The only human to be a captive of the Biters and live to tell the tale.'

Alice felt more than heard something and whispered to the Colonel.

'Should your men have those lights on?'

He replied even as he was putting a scope on his

rifle.

'All of them have night vision scopes like these on their rifles. We are quite safe here.'

Alice was not so sure. Having lived and fought in the woods since she was a child, she knew that in the darkness, victory went not to those with the most firepower but those who knew how to use the darkness to their advantage. The troopers including the Captain seemed to believe, as she had done just days ago, that the Biters would just mindlessly walk in to be slaughtered. But after what she had seen, she wondered if they even knew what they were up against. Something rustled in the dark to her right and a trooper opened fire. Dewan screamed.

'Cease fire till you have a confirmed target!'

Another trooper screamed as a huge shadow leaped out and grabbed him. Alice noticed the floppy hat in the dim light as the trooper screamed while being dragged away into the trees. The other troopers were now firing wildly, and Alice saw that Dewan was now screaming on his radio for the helicopters to come in. More shadows emerged from the trees and two more troopers fell within seconds. Dewan had picked up the light and shone it to his right, revealing a blood-stained trooper who had now crossed over to the Biters and was now walking towards him with his teeth bared. Dewan calmly raised his pistol and put two rounds in the man's head as he asked Alice to pick up a weapon to defend herself. Alice needed no prompting and had a rifle in her hand and was on her knees, waiting as the Biters emerged from the trees. The remaining troopers were huddled in a tight circle and as the Biters came in sight, Alice selected single round mode and put a bullet into one's head. She then sought out another target and brought him down. Dewan was doing the same, and he had shot three Biters in quick succession.

The troopers took courage from Dewan and Alice

and they began firing in a more disciplined way, covering each other, using overlapping fields of fire. As Alice kept squeezing the trigger, she realized this was turning into a slaughter. There were dozens of Biters down now and as others emerged from the trees, it was a matter of seconds before they were cut down.

She heard the sound of helicopters emerging and then the rattle of machine gun fire as one of the helicopter gunships opened fire, scattering the nearest group of Biters, many of them cut to ribbons by the heavy-caliber fire. One helicopter hovered overhead and lowered ropes which the troopers used to climb on board as other helicopters provided covering fire. Alice grabbed the rope when her turn came and then looked into the forest one last time. She thought she caught a glimpse of tall, pointed ears like a rabbit and a frail looking female form next to him. She then heard the Queen scream one last time.

'Alice, remember the truth! Don't believe their lies!'

As she scrambled onto the helicopter, Dewan sat down next to her.

'You're safe now. It's all going to be okay now.'

Alice sat in silence, thinking back to the Queen and everything she had told her.

FIVE

IT WAS THE FIRST TIME Alice had tasted chocolate and she licked the wrapper clean. Food for her had consisted of whatever could be hunted or scavenged. One or two men in their settlement had harbored dreams of growing their own food, but when you're constantly on alert and may have to abandon your position in minutes, you don't really have a lifestyle suited for agriculture. Dewan had walked in and sat down next to Alice. He had showered and changed and was wearing a simple khaki uniform. He seemed to epitomize all the ways in which Zeus was different from the life she had known. He was clean, wearing spotless clothes and was not constantly looking over his back. He seemed to be about the same age as her father, and he asked Alice if she wanted to shower and change before she met anyone else.

Alice was instantly aware of just how she must have looked in the muddy clothes she had worn for the last few days. At the settlement, her mother had gone on and on about how young ladies should always appear well groomed, but when your big extracurricular activity is sniping at Biters and your favorite toy is a handgun, meeting such archaic standards was impossible. Alice's hair was cropped short (so that nobody could grab it in a close fight, as her instructors had said), and her face was lean with her cheekbones showing prominently. She was thin, but certainly not weak, since she had the wiry frame and strength that came with years of running and combat training every day.

After she changed into some khaki clothes Dewan gave her, she joined him in what appeared to be a cafeteria of some sort. There were long benches and tables which were filled with black-clad Zeus troopers. Most of them were men, though Alice did see several women. They all greeted Dewan with deference and he asked her to sit down and ordered dinner. Alice felt her mouth water as hot soup and chicken were put in front of her and Dewan smiled.

'Dig in and don't worry about formalities. You must be starved.'

After that, she needed no more encouragement as she polished off her food. Dewan told her that he would talk more to her the next morning and showed her the way to her room. As Alice was walking to it, she saw two young Zeus troopers looking at her and whispering among themselves. One of them, a young, pimply Indian boy worked up the courage to talk to her.

'Are you the one from the Deadland who lived with the Biters?'

Alice looked him straight in the eye and saw him flinch at her response.

'The Deadland?'

'Oh, you know, the settlements outside our centrally administered zones where people are....'

'Free.'

Alice completed the sentence for him. Her father had told her about how Zeus tried to get more and more settlements into their fold, promising protection in return for the supply of young men and women for their army and effective control over their defenses and supplies. The settlements who signed up got security, but effectively became bonded labour- growing food in farms for Zeus and their masters, giving up their right to bear arms unless Zeus allowed them to, and supplying young men and women to serve in factories and mines that those who controlled Zeus ran. Nobody really knew who the real masters behind Zeus were, but the Queen had mentioned Chinese Red Guards, and she had heard her father sometimes grumble about how he would never submit to the Red Guards.

She walked back to her room, and lay down on what was a simple cot, but a luxury compared to what she had just been through and also compared to the old sleeping bag that was her bed back home. She was fast asleep within seconds of hitting the mattress.

She was awakened by a light tap on the door and she found Dewan standing there, wearing a black uniform.

'Your father is on the way and should be here any time. I thought I'd let you know.'

Alice ran more than walked to the small attached bathroom to shower and change and then joined Dewan in a small meeting room. There were two more men there with him wearing black uniforms covered in medals and badges. One was white and other Indian. The white man, who was bald and built like a bull, spoke first.

'Good morning young lady. My name is General John Appleseed and I oversee all the Asian operations for Zeus. I flew in last night when we learnt that your extraordinary ordeal was coming to an end.'

The Indian, wearing the traditional Sikh turban, spoke next.

'I am Major Balbir Singh. I am in charge of the Indian subcontinent.'

Alice never thought she would get intimidated by any man, but the way these men spoke and the way

Dewan showed deference to them told her just how big and organized Zeus was. That feeling was intensified when her father walked in. He was tall, wiry and wore faded jeans and a crumpled shirt. At first sight one might have assumed that he would be awed by the men in front of him, but he gathered his sobbing daughter in his arms and looked them straight in the eye as he thanked them.

As he began to leave with her, General Appleseed spoke up softly.

'Chief of Mission Gladwell. It is a pleasure to see you after all we have heard of you. It is a pity that you choose not to join your old comrades again.'

Alice felt her father stiffen as he turned to talk to the General. There was a cold bite to his voice, very different from the gentle, loving father she had known.

'General, I served the United States of America and what she stood for- freedom, liberty and equality. That nation is dead, but the spirit lives on in all of us who refuse to bow to the new dictatorship of big business and hired guns and the Chinese tyrants who pay you.'

The General's eyes hardened but his voice remained soft.

'How long can you last out there by yourselves in the Deadland?'

'We've done well so far.'

With those words, he whisked Alice out of the room and walked her out. She wanted to tell him so much about what had happened, but he just hushed her, telling her that they would talk more when they got back. When they stepped out of the building, Alice saw that there was a sprawling air base outside and Dewan ran up behind them.

'Your helicopter is waiting there. Mr. Gladwell, you have an incredibly brave daughter. Good luck to you both.'

Alice's father seemed to size Dewan up for a second and then seemingly liking what he saw, shook his hand, thanking him again as they walked towards the waiting black helicopter. Alice saw four boys whom she recognized from the settlement standing at a far corner. They looked miserable and scared and one of them glared at Alice as she passed him.

'Dad, what are they doing here?'

'They're here to join Zeus as recruits.'

'But we never…'

Her father stopped her.

'That's the price we paid to get you back. Four young, untrained boys for a trained combat veteran like you. We all agreed it was the best decision when Zeus demanded something in return.'

Alice felt like she had been punched in the stomach and felt sick that four boys would now have to live away from their families, in the murky world of the Zeus army because of her. As they sat down in the helicopter, she looked at her father. He looked old and tired, as if he had aged years in just the few days she had been gone. He had implied that the leaders had decided on trading her for the boys, but she knew just how much it must have been gnawing at his own conscience. She reached out and took his arm, and he smiled at her. She saw Dewan waving to them as the helicopter took off and she sat back, wondering just what she had got herself into with that one fateful decision of jumping into that hole behind the bunny eared Biter.

~ * * * ~

Alice's mother smothered her in hugs when she landed and her older sister, Jane, ruffled her hair. That was as close as she had ever seen Jane get to a public display of affection. Jane was almost ten years older than Alice, and remembered enough of what the world had been like before The Rising to harbor bitterness at what she had lost. That bitterness had never entirely left, and if anything, it had acquired an even sharper edge with the years of fighting to survive. For the last one year, they had made an abandoned village their home. The village was located near the crest of a small hill with a great view of all directions, and that made it both easily defensible in case of attack and also offered several escape routes if they had to abandon their settlement.

When Alice walked into the large building that had once been a school but was now the communal dining hall, she could feel many eyes on her. She had been well liked and also respected for her skills, but she saw that something had changed. Many of the men and women she had fought shoulder to shoulder with were averting their gazes. She sat next to Jane, who seemed to be in a foul mood as well.

'What's wrong?'

Jane took a small bite and then answered.

'Everyone's really angry about us giving into Zeus and sending our boys over. They think once Zeus has a foothold they'll be back for more. Some people are saying Dad made the others agree since you were the one involved.'

Alice ate in silence, realizing that whatever she said would not help. She came back to her room and saw that a fresh set of weapons had been laid out for her. Whether they grumbled or not, everyone at the settlement knew that her skills could be needed at any time. She spent the next few hours cleaning her guns and then lay down to sleep. She heard a knock at the door. It was her father.

'Alice, tomorrow some folks from Zeus will be here to take you.'

Alice sat up in a panic, wondering if saving her life had meant sending her to join Zeus as well. Her father saw her expression and sat down next to her.

'No, no. You don't need to worry- I would never let them take you. But they want to question you about what you saw and heard while you were in the Biter base. Nobody's survived so long behind enemy lines and they want to know what you saw. Anything you'd like to tell me before you go with them?'

Alice thought about all that the Queen had said, and even as she began to say something, she realized just how ridiculous it would sound. A Biter Queen who could talk. A supposed conspiracy behind it all led by shadowy powers trying to bring about a New World Order. Biters who were not entirely the bloodthirsty monsters everyone took them for. Whichever way she tried to spin it, she thought it made her sound crazy or delusional. So she just shrugged and lay down to rest and was asleep within seconds.

She was awakened by the sound of helicopter rotors and when she sat up, she saw her parents standing near her.

'Sweetheart, they're here to get you. They promised us that you'd be back by evening. Just tell them whatever they want to know and you'll be fine.'

Despite his reassuring words, Alice could see the strain in her father's eyes. She knew that he was dealing with a lot of compromises he had been forced to make to get her back- sending the boys to Zeus and dealing with those he had tried hard to avoid all these years. He had often told Alice that unlike before The Rising when there was at least some form of order due to governments, the chaos and vacuum that had resulted had been filled by greedy, power-hungry men and their private armies. He had spent all these years keeping their settlement free of such men and now to protect his daughter, he had been forced to compromise with them. Alice was old enough to realize just how much of a sacrifice her father had made for her and she hugged him tight as she boarded the black helicopter.

The helicopter turned North East, and flew over forests on the outskirts of what had once been Delhi, but was now simply called the Ruins. On her previous flights she had been too terrified or tired to notice, but now she got her first look from the air at what lay below. It was a depressingly familiar pattern- miles upon miles of wrecked buildings and debris, broken by the occasional small settlement of humans. Without many standing buildings, the sands from the Rajasthan deserts were now freely swirling over the cities nearby, creating a near constant haze.

She then saw a large fortified compound with gun turrets on the walls, followed by the airfield she had seen before. As the helicopter came to a rest, she saw Dewan run up to it. While he was a stranger by any standards, he was the one familiar face and she felt a bit more comfortable having him there. He spoke loudly to be heard over the helicopters and Alice leaned over to hear what he was saying.

'General Appleseed himself is here. From what I gather, what our Intelligence folks most want is tactical intel. So just tell them what happened when you went into the Biter base, what you saw, the numbers of Biters and so on. Also, any clues as to where hidden entrances could be will be very helpful. That's really all they want, so it should be pretty simple and then you're on your way home.'

It sounded simple enough and Alice was feeling much more reassured when she stepped into the briefing room. General Appleseed was the only one there and as Dewan saluted, he asked him and Alice to sit down. The big General folded his arms in front of him and smiled, trying to put Alice at ease. With his big neck, huge arms and bald head, it was hard to think of the General as anything other than a raging bull, but Alice smiled back, glad that he was at least trying to be nice.

'Ms. Gladwell..'

He paused, puzzled as Alice stifled a laugh.

'I'm sorry, nobody's ever called me Ms. Gladwell

before.'

Appleseed grinned and continued.

'Okay, Alice. I know you've had a tough few days, but you know just how terrible our continuing war is, and any information that can help us strike a blow for all humans would be of great value.'

Alice didn't say anything, but she noted that Zeus was now claiming to represent all humans. She wondered what her father would have said to that as the General continued.

'So, please just let me know everything you saw and experienced. Don't worry about any detail seeming to be too small or insignificant, just tell me everything from the beginning.'

So Alice began her tale, starting with how she had seen a Biter jump down a hole and how she had followed. She watched Appleseed raise his eyebrows as she talked about the first confrontation in the caves and how she had managed to get away. He was scribbling notes furiously and stopped when she mentioned about the room she had entered and the seal she had seen on the door. He looked at Dewan.

'That can only be where the US Embassy was. I know we had underground bunkers, but who would have thought those mindless monsters would have used our own underground bunkers and the ones the Indians had built against nukes to hide? When we're done here, I'd like a recon group to go and check out the area.'

Alice continued her story, about how she managed to get into the room and saw old newspapers. When Appleseed asked what was on those papers, Alice replied that she saw the pictures of when The Rising first happened, but that she could not read fast enough. She thought she saw a flicker of satisfaction cross Appleseed's face as he continued.

'Now these creatures were outside the door. How did you manage to get out?'

Alice started speaking and then wondered how she could possibly explain the drawing on the wall and why the Biters did not tear her apart or at any rate bite her to convert her into one of them. However, she had never been a good liar, and struggled with what she should tell the General. Her dilemma was solved when a trooper knocked on the door.

'Sir, we are serving lunch in the cafeteria now. Will you come and join us or should I send it over here?'

Appleseed growled, his friendly demeanor gone in an instant.

'Trooper, we're working here! Colonel, can you ask them to arrange a bite here?'

Dewan walked out, resting a friendly hand on Alice's shoulder as he left. Alice looked back to see Appleseed looking at her with his chin in his hands, as if contemplating something. Finally he came around the table to sit next to Alice.

'Alice, we will continue the debriefing when Dewan gets here, but there is one thing I needed to ask you in private. It is a highly confidential matter that nobody else should know about, but if you helped me with this, it could make a huge difference to the war effort.'

He took out a photograph from his pocket and put it on the table in front of Alice. It was an old, faded photo, with some of the edges torn off, but the smiling face with greying hair in the middle of it was unmistakable. It was the woman whom Alice had met as the Queen. She tried to contain her reaction, but Appleseed must have noticed.

'Alice, I need you to tell me if you saw this woman.'

~ * * * ~

Alice was saved from having to answer by Dewan coming in with some sandwiches. As they ate, Alice told them about how after the encounter in the Embassy room, she had managed to hide in the underground caves and tunnels for the next two days. Appleseed was skeptical and his expression showed it.

'When our men first saw you, it seems you were in the company of Biters. How did that happen?'

Alice's mind raced. At the best of times, she was terrible at making up excuses, now she had to find some plausible reason for why the Biters around her had not attacked her when they first encountered the Zeus helicopters.

'General, I was hiding behind some ruins when your helicopters arrived. The Biters would have found me in minutes if they had not landed up when they did. I was hardly with the Biters then- but with all the fighting, I couldn't get to the troopers and I hid underground.'

'And what about the incident in the forest when we gave you the beacon? Or did you again just happen to be near the Biters? One of our men said that it looked like they had you in their custody.'

Alice saw that Appleseed was not going to be so easily convinced.

'Biters can hardly take anyone in their custody. They tried to get me in the forest and I was fighting them off when your men arrived. It was all so chaotic that someone must have mistakenly believed the Biters had captured me. I was scared and in the middle of so many Biters that I just dove into one of the openings in the ground. It seemed to lead into one of their bases and I hid there, waiting for you guys to get me.'

Dewan nodded at Appleseed and whispered that he had indeed seen her fighting Biters when he first saw her. The General just grunted as Alice continued her tale about how she had been deep underground escaping the Biters when the rescue mission was mounted. As she talked, she noticed that the General seemed to be relaxing a bit as he clearly got pieces of information that he deemed useful, such as the exact location of the tunnels near the old Yamuna river, and more than once he whispered to Dewan to get sorties out over the areas to check them out for any sign of Biters. Finally he closed the writing pad in front of him and asked Dewan to go and check if the helicopter to fly Alice back had been arranged.

As Dewan left the room, Appleseed was again right beside Alice, the photo in his hand.

'Alice, in my time I've interrogated many men and women, and I know that you're keeping something from me.'

He reached over and gripped Alice's knee hard, and then Alice felt his hand moving up her leg.

'In my time, we had many ways of persuading young, attractive women like you to co-operate.'

Alice cringed as the General's hand moved higher and then on instinct, she grabbed his hand with her left hand, and just as her instructors had taught her, she twisted it and brought her right palm hard against the flat of his hand. Appleseed's hand snapped back and he howled in pain as Alice stood up, ready to fight. The General towered over her and outweighed her by a big margin, but Alice's parents had not brought her up to give in so easily. She would go down fighting if need be. Appleseed was holding his wrist and his face was red.

'I should have known better than to reason with a wild girl from the Deadland like you. Savages like you aren't fit to be with humans any more. The days of isolated settlements are going to be a thing of the past- and you need to learn how to live in human society again.'

Alice spat on the ground, knowing that there was no need to waste her effort on being polite any more.

'So that we can be slaves to you and your masters, whoever they are? Is the war against the Biters your mission or is that an excuse to get power?'

Appleseed smiled.

'The woman whose photo I showed you is a known traitor and a Biter sympathizer. We know that she lives among them and claims to be some sort of leader. We don't let that information get out because we don't want anyone to know that the Biters can be lived with after all. She is a traitor and the Central Committee has already condemned her to death. Anyone collaborating with her is also a traitor.'

Alice didn't flinch at the threat.

'I have no idea who she is, but it looks like you are the ones who are keeping secrets. How would your men feel if they knew that the Biters could actually co-exist with us, and that your war is based on lies.'

Alice regretted what she said next a second after the words left her mouth, but she was angry and wanted to lash out, to see Appleseed on the defensive.

'I cannot read fast, but I can read, and in the rooms below, I saw papers that I had lots of time to read. Papers that talked about experiments done before The Rising, about how the Great Fires were wars waged by elements in human governments to get power, about how people could have been vaccinated if your masters wanted to.'

Appleseed looked as if he had been punched in the gut, but then he smiled, not a smile born out of good humor, but that of a predator looking at a helpless prey.

'Your friend Dr. Protima had tried to reach out to her associates in the early days, telling them such stories and I personally had the pleasure of breaking many of them. I never got her but I managed to stamp out these lies. My masters have been working for years to create a new Earth, one where there is no overpopulation, no poverty, no weakness. They selected those who were to be vaccinated and we would have repopulated our cities and started afresh. The spread of the infection and the way it mutated surprised us, but we would have achieved what we wanted long ago by wiping out those critters had it not been for that stubborn hag.'

Alice was suddenly very afraid. There was only one reason Appleseed could be sharing all this so openly- if he had no fear that she could give away these secrets. He loomed over her.

'And you, my dear, a wild girl from an inconsequential settlement, ruled by that delusional, idealistic father of yours. Do you think you can come in the way of the vision of the most powerful men in the world? The Central Committee is based in China, but unlike what your father believes, it's not just the Chinese. Elements of the Chinese government of old are there, together with the richest and most powerful bankers and politicians of the Old World. You are like an insect before their vision for a New World.'

He heard the door open as Dewan came back and he leaned close and whispered.

'Be careful, my dear. Accidents are known to happen all the time in the Deadland where you live.'

Alice walked to the helicopter, numb with fear and dreading what was to follow. A part of her had wanted to believe that the Queen's rants and prophecies were nothing more than the product of a delusional mind. She had wanted nothing more than to forget about all that she had seen and heard while she had been among the Biters and to get on with her life. To have Appleseed so casually admit that it was all true chilled her. There was of course the realization that perhaps everything the Queen had said had been true after all, and that perhaps the Biters were not the only, or even the most dangerous enemies ordinary people like Alice and her family had to fear. As the helicopter took off, she saw Appleseed standing on the flight line, waving to her.

Her first thought was that she would go and tell her father everything. She didn't know if he would believe her, but she was sure that he would have some ideas on what to do. After all, what could she do alone against someone like Appleseed, his masters, and all the force Zeus could bring to bear? Between the hordes of Biters who regarded every human with fear and hatred and Zeus, what chance did she have alone?

Then an even greater fear gripped her. Appleseed had known who her father was. He would know that she would likely go and tell him everything. She suddenly felt very afraid for what the coming days were going to bring for her and her settlement.

SIX

ALICE HAD A QUIET DINNER back at the settlement, but found it impossible to sleep. Jane was lying in her own sleeping bag just feet from her, and Alice considered waking her up, but then dismissed the thought. What could she possibly tell her older sister that would make the story she had to tell sound anything other than ludicrous? She lay in silence for a few more minutes, but soon realized that she was so on edge that there was no way she could sleep. Her ears seemed to be picking up every sound and magnifying it, mirroring her fears. A solitary footstep sounded like a full squad of Zeus troopers, the sound of a bird or bat flying made her wonder if a helicopter was on the way. Finally, Alice sat up and realized that the risk of her being laughed at or not believed was nothing compared to what would happen if Appleseed did carry out his threat and the settlement was taken totally by surprise.

She got up and quietly walked to the room her parents were in. Her mother was asleep, but her father was poring over some papers. The brutal fact was that everyone who had survived so long in the Deadland had to know how to take a life, and she knew her father had done his share of fighting and killing, but he always was more in his element as a man of peace. Which was why he was the de facto leader of their settlement. He was the person people knew they could rely on to get fair advice on how to solve a dispute. He was the one who was trusted to tally and apportion their stocks of food and fuel, which he was doing now. And he was the only person in the world whom Alice could contemplate trusting with her secret.

He looked up at Alice and smiled, motioning for her to sit down next to him.

'Dad, can we talk outside?'

He put the papers aside and joined her in the chill of the night. As they walked together around the settlement, he didn't say a word, choosing to wait for when Alice would be ready to say what was on her mind.

'Dad, I think I found out some stuff. It sounds crazy, but I think it's true and because of it, we may all be in danger. I'm really scared.'

He stopped and looked at her.

'Alice, all those years ago when everything suddenly went to hell, I was just as scared. Your Mom was expecting you and with all the chaos in the last few days, I had no idea how I could protect my family.'

'So what did you do?'

He smiled, the light from torches burning around the settlement's walls reflecting in his glasses.

'I got help. Sometimes the bravest thing you can do is to ask for help. I went to a General in the Indian Army who had become a friend, and he let us shelter with his unit in their barracks when the Biters came out. He and I started this settlement once we had to leave the cities after they became unlivable and we realized that there was no more government and no more help coming our way.'

Alice wrapped her hands around herself, not just because of the chill, but because she needed to brace herself to tell her story. Her father put an arm around her and they continued walking as she spoke. He didn't interrupt her once, though he did see his face cloud over with a flash of anger when she related what had happened with Appleseed.

Finally, he stopped and seemed to be staring off into the distance. When he said nothing for several seconds, Alice tugged at his hand.

'Dad, I know it sounds crazy. That's why I was so afraid of saying anything to you.'

When her father turned to look at her, Alice was shocked to see his eyes well up with tears.

'Alice, when the first infections emerged and within a day or two all law and order broke down, a lady had come to meet me at the Embassy, pleading with me to pass on some information to my superiors in Washington. The Ambassador was in the US so she wanted to meet me. Just before she was to come and visit me, I got a call direct from someone in the White House that I was not to meet her or to entertain anything she had to say. I thought she was another wacko who had lost it in the madness of those days and I did not meet her.'

Alice felt her heart almost stop as she guessed what was to come next.

'That lady's name was Dr. Protima Dasgupta. She was an Indian-American researcher who had recently left the Government. My background check showed that she had been working on some Classified projects, which had such a high level of secrecy that I couldn't even find out what they were.'

'So everything she said is....'

Her father exhaled loudly, as if clearing his mind and trying to come to grips with what he now faced.

'Alice, I don't know if everything she said is true or not, but what's clear based on what you saw is that there is more to the Biters than we've always been led to believe. In the five days after The Rising when the media was still on, did you know what was on TV every single day?'

Alice had never watched TV but knew of it from her parents and sister so she just shook her head.

'Reports about how horrible these creatures, these mutants were. Reports about how our brave troops were fighting a new war on terror. Every single channel was screaming about how these creatures needed to be wiped out. But what was funny was that ordinary folks had no real protection- most National Guard units in the US were pulled back to barracks. Then all of a sudden, wars started breaking out all over. If I were a conspiracy nut, which I most certainly am not, I could start connecting all those dots and say that what this Queen or Dr. Protima has to say may well be more true than not. But that's not what worries me most. Something else terrifies me.'

'What, Dad?'

He looked at Alice, his eyes dead serious.

'Till Protima lives, there is a chance that this secret could come out, and getting to her is the only chance Zeus and its masters have of wiping out the Biters as per their plan and then bring the surviving humans under their control. Appleseed now suspects that you know where she may be. He will be coming for you.'

Alice tried to put on a brave face.

'Dad, can we hold them? We have almost two hundred men and women who can fight. We can all shoot well, and we know this area better than they ever will.'

He shook his head sadly.

'No, sweetheart, we won't be able to hold them. You've seen a lot more death and evil than I would have ever wished upon a child of mine, but the most evil thing in this world is what one man can do to another. If Zeus comes here with their air power and heavy weapons, we won't last more than a few minutes. They will wipe us out and take you away.'

Alice didn't know what to say. Part of her felt guilty for having involved her father. The rational part of her knew that the dangers would have been just as great and just as real even if she had not told a soul, but telling her father and seeing how scared even he seemed made it even more real, and infinitely more frightening.

~ * * * ~

'Gladwell, we don't know if even a word of this is true.'

The speaker was Rajiv, a former banker who had become one of the pillars of their settlement ever since he and his wife had stumbled onto them while running from a horde of Biters. Alice had sat quietly for the half hour her father had taken to relate her story. He had thankfully spared her the ordeal of having to speak in front of more than two hundred people, most of whom looked increasingly skeptical as the tale progressed. Alice saw more than a few of them get up and leave. She knew they were among the many who had lost family and friends to the Biters, and even an insinuation that the Biters were anything but a mindless, bloodthirsty horde offended them. What made it worse was that the first accusation came not from one of the rabble-rousers but the normally placid Rajiv.

Alice's father looked at Rajiv, pleading with him.

'Why on Earth would Alice make all this up?'

Rajiv looked sheepish and shrugged his shoulders.

'She is but a girl. Maybe she just got scared in the tunnels down there and imagined things.'

'Or maybe this is just you trying to hold onto your so-called freedom!'

That stinging accusation came from the rear of the group, and Alice saw her father flinch as if he had been struck physically. His accuser was now standing up, and as three or four more men stood up, felt emboldened to continue his tirade.

'For years, Zeus has been coming to us. What they want isn't much- our boys to join their army, a share of whatever we find by way of salvage and maintaining a tally of our weapons with them. In return, we get some fixed rations, ammunition and safety.'

Alice saw her father's face tighten.

'We are FREE! That counts for something. We all owed allegiance to others, and several of you served in Government or in uniform, so we all know what that meant. But that was different- that was allegiance to a nation, to our identity. Zeus are a bunch of hired guns, and their real masters never reveal themselves openly. Have you forgotten about those settlements who signed up and then had their weapons taken because Zeus decided they were needed elsewhere? Who saved them from attacks after that? What about those who were re-settled into farms to grow food, half of which is taken away by Zeus for their masters with no payment. What about all those young people who are taken away and never seen again- and the rumors that they are being used as bonded labour in the factories and mines of the elites who control Zeus. Why become their slaves when we can be free?'

It was an old argument, one that had consumed many meetings before, but tonight the revelations about what Alice had found had given it a new, bitter edge. The man who had been arguing with her father refused to back down.

'We all know how you feel about it, and you also know that there have been some of us who disagree. Some of us who are tired of fighting to survive every day, or scavenging for food every day for our families. And now you conveniently have this fairy tale from your daughter where Zeus and their masters are some sort of super-villains who destroyed the world.'

As the meeting disbanded, Alice's father took her

aside.

'I tried, sweetheart, but their minds are closed. The problem is that if this General is indeed going to strike, we are running out of time. We cannot just sit here and debate and hope we convince these people.'

'Dad, what can we do?'

He hesitated, as if weighing in his mind whether to say what was on his mind.

'We need to meet this Dr. Protima. She's the only one who could convince them.'

Alice shuddered at the thought of going back to the Biters in their dank, dark underground world, and also of what they would do to her when they found her after her betrayal.

'Dad, I don't know if what they said is true or not, but that silly prophecy and that book she has freaks me out.'

'Darling, that's just an old fairy tale called Alice in Wonderland. I don't blame her if she has lost her mind a bit down there and believes it to be some prophecy. I guess they heard your name and saw the way you met them, and wanted to believe it was this prophecy come true, that's all. If that's what it takes to save us all, then just play along for a little bit.'

Alice could see her father's conflicted face, because he knew he was putting her in harm's way. But the sheer fact that he was willing to even contemplate that told her just how desperate their situation was.

The next morning, Alice walked along the woods where she had followed Bunny Ears down the hole. They were a good five miles away from their settlement, and if there was trouble, they would not be able to make it back in time, and of course, there was no way they could expect help or reinforcements. Alice held a pistol in her right hand and a shotgun slung across her back, but she had already seen that up close, with the weight of numbers on their side, the firepower she carried would count for little if the Biters were intent on attacking her. Her father was sitting a hundred meters away, hidden in the trees, his face daubed with camouflage paint, his eyes glued to the scope of his rifle.

Alice had no idea if Bunny Ears or any other Biter would even show up again at this location, but as far as she knew, no other human had found this entrance, and now that she scanned the area, it was so well hidden that she could not spot it either. So if it had not been compromised, there was a chance that they would still be using it. Also, she reminded herself, they were probably looking for her. That thought made her grip the handgun in her hand even tighter as she waited.

They waited for what seemed to be an eternity, and as Alice was about to give up and go to her father and ask if they should just return to the settlement, she saw some movement in the bushes. She froze, both hands gripping the handgun, but she forced herself to not bring the gun up. If their plan was to work, she had to make sure that she was not seen as a threat. She held her breath as the bushes parted, reassured by the fact that at this very moment her father's rifle would be trained on whatever was emerging. She saw two pointy ears emerge first, and then Bunny Ears was in front of her. He growled, spitting in her direction, and for a moment, Alice thought that he was about to attack. He pounded his feet on the ground and raised his head to the skies, howling, but as Alice watched she realized that his roar was not one of fury but more a plaintive wail.

She tucked her handgun into her belt and took a step closer. As she looked at Bunny Ears, she saw that he too was looking at her with his lifeless eyes. She had no idea if he would understand what she wanted, but she had no other choice. She spoke in a gentle voice.

'I am so sorry. I did not know what Zeus and their

masters were up to, and I did not believe the Queen. I know now, and I need your help. The only way we can survive is if we help each other. Please tell the Queen that I need her help. We've tried convincing others in the settlement but many of them don't believe us.'

Bunny Ears just looked at her for a few seconds and then he disappeared back into the bushes. Alice wondered if he had understood a single word she had said.

~ * * * ~

Alice was sleeping with her shotgun near her head, and her parents had insisted that she and her sister sleep in the same room as them. It was hard to believe that things had got so bad so fast. It had begun with a fight between two young boys at lunch-time, one of them supporting her father and another insisting that they should just go the way of so many other settlements and do what Zeus wanted. When things had got more personal and some harsh words had been said about Alice, a couple of her friends had waded in. Soon words had given way to blows and before anyone could control it, the settlement had been neatly divided down the middle. What was apparent was that it had to do with more than whether they believed Alice's story, or even what they thought about joining Zeus. It had become a battle for power. A battle between Alice's father and some of the original founders of the settlement and others who had joined them more recently, and resented the authority the old-timers wielded.

Alice's father would have normally waved it all off as yet another of the countless arguments that had been inevitable over the years when you put strangers together in such a high-stress situation. But now things were different. He knew the imminent danger of Zeus moving against them, and he had also now seen first-hand that what Alice had said had some truth to it. He had been tempted to pull the trigger the moment he saw the Biter emerge in front of his daughter, and he had to fight years of conditioning to not blow his head away. But then he had seen it stand there, apparently listening, apparently understanding, and then walking away. With all the devastation the world had endured, if there was even a small chance that things could be set right, then it was worth fighting for.

He had called a meeting just after breakfast and as the entire settlement gathered, he noticed that the lines were drawn. People were sitting in groups, and those he knew supported his views were sitting around him and his family. However, an even larger group was now sitting around Rajiv, who had somehow taken on leadership of the splinter group. Better him than one of the rabble-rousers, he thought, as he began his account of what he had seen.

He was less than a minute into it when he saw the dissenters stirring. Rajiv stood up.

'Gladwell, we go way back, but you cannot seriously expect us to believe this. I understand you're trying to help your daughter but this is too incredible to be true. After all the Biters have done to us, why are you doing this?'

He heard a few catcalls and a man's voice boomed out from the crowd.

'He's just scared of no longer being the head honcho if we join Zeus, that's all. And if he hates Zeus so much why did he strike a deal to save his daughter?'

Alice could see her father wither in the face of the criticism and he put his head down, defeated, knowing that nothing he could say was going to make a difference.

Just then one of the lookouts shouted.

'There's an intruder headed our way.'

Immediately, all differences were forgotten as guns were picked up, safeties switched off and men and women began taking their defensive positions. Those too young, old or sick to fight were herded to the middle of the village to shelter in the building that served as their communal dining hall. Everyone else was expected to fight. Alice was one of the first to reach the wall where the shout had come from, and she was on top of the boxes that served as the perch for snipers before many of the older and slower men had even reached the wall. She put her rifle to her shoulders and peered through the sniper scope. She could hear others take position around her and the nervous shuffling and swearing of those who had not seen combat before. As Alice waited, she found a clarity that had eluded her in the confusion of the last few days. This was what she had been trained to do since she could walk. This was when there was no ambiguity to deal with- where it was simple- kill or be killed. A familiar adrenaline rush washed over her, and she welcomed it, waiting for a target to present itself.

'Alice, got something on your scope?'

Alice grinned and asked the man to wait. It was one of the men who had been heckling her father just minutes ago. It was reassuring to know that they still realized and respected the fact that Alice was one of the best shots in the settlement.

'Ram, did you actually see anything or were you drinking more of your hooch again last night?'

That question from Alice's father brought laughter all around and helped to lessen some of the tension. Alice was still too young to fully grasp it, but she had an intuitive understanding of just why so many men and women had followed her father over the years. It was not because he was the strongest or even the bravest, but because he could keep people calm in a crisis, he could think when others were losing their heads. She peered through her scope once again and this time she saw someone emerging from the early morning mist. As the figure resolved itself, she saw someone covered in a full-length coat, one that seemed several sizes too big, and walking towards their settlement at a steady, almost leisurely pace. She moved the scope up and caught her breath as she realized who was approaching. It was Dr.Protima, or as she preferred to be called nowadays, the Queen of the Biters.

Alice heard one or two rifles being cocked so she called out.

'Hold your fire. It's just an old woman.'

Two men from the settlement unlocked the gate and went out, cautiously approaching the figure who was now just a hundred meters away. Alice watched them trade some words and then heaved a sigh of relief when they led her in.

When the Queen walked in through the gate, every man, woman and child in the settlement had gathered to see who this stranger was. In the early days they had often encountered solitary stragglers, but by now, people were either in groups, or dead. A single person, least of all an old woman, had virtually no chance of surviving on their own in the Deadland. Alice saw that the Queen had prepared well. The oversized coat covered her body and arms, and she wore long gloves to conceal her hands. She was wearing tinted glasses that obscured her eyes and as she came in, she glanced towards Alice once, but betrayed no hint of recognition.

As someone offered her a chair, she sat down and said that she had to talk to someone in charge. When Alice's father and some of the other men sat around her, she looked around at the dozens of people gathered around her, perhaps waiting for them to leave. But there was no chance of that happening- the entire settlement wanted to know what this strange old woman had to say. And then she began her tale.

'My name is Dr. Protima and I was a Biologist of Indian origin who lived and worked in the United States for several years.'

Alice saw her father's eyes widen as he realized who she was, and saw several of the men stir, but they all sat and listened. And the Queen had indeed come prepared to meet a skeptical audience. Under the coat, she had a small bag from which she produced old faded passports, identity cards, official documents bearing the seal of the US Government. Some of the younger folks would not know what many of those were, but were suitably impressed, but all the older ones, the ones who had known a life before The Rising, saw and understood. Alice saw some of the men who had been opposed to her father pass the documents among each other, and saw several of them glance at her.

Rajiv finally worked up the courage to speak, when the Queen concluded her tale, ending with how Alice had landed in their midst.

'Dr. Protima, we have heard some of this before from Alice, and it still seems incredible. How can we believe any of this?'

She did not say a single word in reply, but stood up and loosened the coat so it fell at her feet. Then she took off her gloves and glasses and looked straight at Rajiv. There were gasps all around her, and one or two women screamed. Rajiv stumbled back, holding onto another man for support as he looked into the decayed, lifeless eyes and the yellowing, bloodied arms of the Queen. No one said anything for a few seconds, and then Alice's father spoke.

'Dr. Protima, if this vaccine got into the right hands, could it save any more humans from being...'

As he fumbled with what to say, she answered.

'Yes. It would ensure that no more humans have to worry about the virus being transmitted through a bite. Imagine what that would do to the chances of people finally coming to grips with the fact that we are not just dangerous animals and an existential threat to be wiped out? What would that do to Zeus's fear-mongering which they are using to wipe us out and bring all of you under their control?'

Alice heard many murmurs of approval in the crowd, as the Queen now looked straight at her.

'But there's more than that. Before it all went out of control, we were working on antidotes, not just vaccines. If I can get the vaccine to a good lab, we should be able to create a cure. It may take time, but I know it can be done. I don't know how much brain damage has already happened to those infected, or whether it can be reversed, but there is at least hope. Alice, I told you my prophecy was what would lead us to a way out.'

Nobody else present understood what she meant by the last comment, but they were all looking at Alice with a mixture of shame and awe. They had doubted and rejected her, but now they had proof before their eyes that she had been right. Moreover, they suddenly found themselves the bearers of a terrible secret. Many people began speaking at once, everyone with their own idea on what to do, but everyone in agreement that they needed to help get the vaccine into the right hands.

Alice's father spoke next and what he said stunned everyone into silence.

'The men who caused all this will not let us succeed so easily. We know they have been hunting Dr. Protima and now they will come for us.'

Nobody said anything for a few seconds. Alice was about to say something when the silence was shattered by the sound of an incoming helicopter.

SEVEN

EVERYONE AT THE SETTLEMENT WAS watching, most down the sights of their guns as the black helicopter landed at the foot of the hill leading to their village. Alice had her sniper rifle at her shoulder and while many of the younger kids were babbling about this being an attack, she knew better. If Zeus had wanted to launch an attack, they would have come from the skies, raining rockets and bombs from high above, while Alice and the others at her settlement would have been impotent to do anything about it. By landing the helicopter in such a vulnerable position, whoever was coming was indicating that they came in peace, at least for now.

Alice put down her rifle to motion to some of the men behind her to not get trigger happy and wait for her signal before doing anything. When she looked back towards the helicopter, she did not need her sights to know who was coming. The imposing bulk and bald head of the uniformed man now making his way up the hill told her who it was.

Why would Appleseed be coming alone? Alice had spent the last few days in the fear that he would lash out with an unexpected attack, so why was he coming here like this?

When he reached the gates of the settlement, Alice's father asked for the gates to be opened and Appleseed walked into the midst of two hundred armed, scared and jittery people.

'Gladwell, tell your people I pose no threat. You can all see that I am unarmed.'

Appleseed held up his hands to reinforce the point, but even that did little to defuse the tension. Everyone at the settlement had heard about Alice's adventures and the threats this General had made, and none of them was willing to take his words at face value. Appleseed looked around, and seeing Alice, he smiled and said through gritted teeth.

'So young Alice, we meet again.'

Alice spat in his direction, and several people jeered. Appleseed didn't seem to be ruffled and addressed Alice's father.

'Gladwell, your daughter has grown up in the Deadland, so I don't blame her, but you were a diplomat. Surely, you can sit down and talk in a civilized manner with an unarmed guest?'

Alice's father lifted the shotgun he was carrying, casually aiming it at Appleseed's ample gut.

'Any bastard who threatens my daughter is no guest at my home.'

All trace of civility dissipated from Appleseed's face as he pulled a chair and sat down, staring at Alice's father with undisguised hatred.

'Fine, let's play it your way. Give me Dr. Protima and all of you can go on with your miserable lives.'

There was a stunned silence and as Alice's father started to say something, Appleseed cut him off.

'Don't waste my time. I've had unmanned drones watching your settlement ever since your darling daughter spilled the beans on her freak friend. So I know she's here. I just want her handed over. Oh yes, as per the rules laid out by the Central Committee, all of you are guilty of treason for collaborating with the Biter enemy, and I could have all of you executed for it. Instead, I'll settle for confiscating all your weapons and relocating you to one of our safe zones.'

There was a commotion among the group as Alice's father roared in anger.

'This Central Committee of your, these rich men who hide in their bases together with the Chinese tyrants, do not rule us. They rule only their hired dogs like you, and what they say or want has no jurisdiction here. As for Dr. Protima, you have no authority here to take anyone away.'

Appleseed stayed calm, knowing that he held all the cards.

'One air strike is all it would take to turn all of you into smoking carcasses. Tempting as that is, I need that witch alive. That is the only reason I am sitting here and not sifting through your corpses after an air strike. The Central Committee has to make sure that she is not capable of spreading her lies and that we know where her hidden bases are. This is your last chance before you officially commit an act of treason.'

Alice saw Rajiv look at her father, and she wondered if there would be those who would be willing to give into Appleseed's demands. After all, how many of them would risk their lives and their families for an old lady with an incredible tale? Alice's father was perhaps thinking the same thing and he spoke aloud, addressing all those in the settlement.

'For years, we have lived a life that is little more than surviving from day to day. We have taught out children nothing more than how to kill and avoid being killed. All of us who lived before The Rising know that there is more to life than that. I had forgotten that life and I had resigned myself to a life where my only and biggest achievement was to see my family live one more day. But today, I realized there is hope. There is hope that the evil that has overtaken all our lives can be reversed. There is hope that once again we can live like humans, not wild animals. That hope is worth fighting for, and I for one will not give into someone who represents the same forces that destroyed all our lives in the first place. I will not choose for you. If you choose not to side with me, I will take my family and those with me and leave with Dr. Protima.'

Appleseed snorted derisively.

'His daughter filled your ears with fairy tales, and you have this delusional old woman who means nothing to any of you. Why throw away your lives for them?'

Rajiv walked up to Appleseed and looked him in the eye.

'When I was a banker, I thought the bloody stock market crashing was the end of the world. If there's one positive of all this crap we've gone through, it's that it has given me a sense of perspective, a sense of what really matters and what is worth standing up for. I will stand by the men and women who sheltered me when I had nothing and whom I have fought with shoulder to shoulder every day. You can stuff your Central Committee up your fat ass.'

If Alice's father's appeal had not done the trick, Rajiv's certainly did and everyone gathered started cheering. Alice walked up to Appleseed and tapped him on the shoulder.

'I don't think you're welcome here any more.'

He glared at her and began to walk away, when the Queen emerged from the building where she had been hiding and stood next to Alice.

'General, wait. I believe you were looking for me.'

He stopped in his tracks and turned to look at her, and then recoiled in horror as she took off her glasses and gloves.

'I dare say General, for a delusional old woman I still have a bit of a bite.'

As she opened and snapped shut her bloody teeth,

92

Appleseed stumbled back, almost falling down as he realized what the true nature of the elusive Dr. Protima he had been pursuing for so many years was. He ran more than walked out of the gate, as cheers rang out all around Alice. The Queen looked around her and spoke to no one in particular.

'There is still goodness left in man. There is indeed still hope.'

Alice's father shouted above the cheering.

'Quiet everyone! We've done enough celebrating, now we need to get ready.'

'For what?' shouted someone in the crowd.

'For the attack that is surely on its way even as we speak.'

~ * * * ~

Alice watched till the combination of the smoke drifting into her eyes and her own tears made it impossible for her to see much more. Jane was tugging at her arm and shouting something, but Alice did not hear a word of what she was saying. All she heard was the crackling sound of what had been her home for more than a year burn down to the ground. And yes, the sound of men screaming. Men she had trained with, men she had known all her life. Above all else, the one man she had loved with all her heart- her father.

Soon after Appleseed had left, Alice's father had asked for twenty volunteers to stay on in the settlement, both to slow down the Zeus forces that were surely on their way, and also to ensure that any drones watching them didn't spot that they were in fact abandoning their settlement. Alice had bawled and pleaded when it was obvious that her father would stay. He had just held her tight and spoke to her as she cried.

'Alice, you must survive. Dr. Protima and her secret

must survive. Just remember that and while you are young, you must now lead the ones who remain.'

The remaining people half-crouched, half-crawled through the narrow irrigation tunnels behind the settlement. Alice's father had them covered long ago, thinking they would provide a good place to hide or to make a quiet getaway, and now they were being put to use as Alice, her mother, sister, Dr. Protima and the others made for the neighboring forests. It was from there that Alice saw the attack unfold. Three black helicopters swept in low and took positions, hovering just meters above the settlement. Appleseed was in one of them, and Alice could hear his voice booming over a loudspeaker, offering one last chance for surrender. When there was no response, Zeus troopers began rappelling out of the helicopters. For a split second, Alice's heart had harbored hopes that her father and the other men may make it when their first volley brought down several of the Zeus troopers. But then she realized both just how cruel, and how merciless Appleseed was. He had sacrificed his first men as pawns to make the defenders reveal their positions. Three more helicopters, sleek, fast gunships, swept in, raking the settlement with rockets and machine guns. A brutal, hammering assault than ended when more than half the buildings in the settlement were ablaze and all defending guns silent.

Another wave of Zeus troopers landed, but Alice saw that her father had more tricks up his sleeve. She watched through tear-filled eyes as several jury-rigged bombs, mostly cans filled with fuel, were set off, making the Zeus troopers dive for cover and a single sniper rifle barked several times from the second floor of the building where Alice's parents had lived. Two Zeus troopers fell and didn't get up. Four troopers tried to rush the building, but two more were brought down by sniper fire. Finally a helicopter fired two rockets that destroyed the building as Alice screamed in agony.

More Zeus troopers entered the settlement, and started going door to door. When it was obvious that most of the residents had abandoned the settlement, Alice saw them signal frantically to the hovering helicopters. She knew that she could wait no longer. Her throat burned and she longed to strike out at the men who had just killed her father, but she remembered what her father had told her. Most of the combat tested veterans had chosen to stay behind at the settlement, choosing to go down fighting so that their families may have a chance. Of the ones left, leave aside a couple of men who were good shots, Alice was perhaps the most experienced in both battle and in navigating the woods. She now had to lead them to safety. In the confusion of the hasty flight into the woods, she had lost sight of the Queen, and only hoped that she had not abandoned the humans who had sacrificed so much to keep her and her cause alive.

It was now nearly dark, and they could no longer hear the helicopters at the settlement. That could mean only one thing- that Appleseed had realized that pursuing them from the air was of no use in the dark when they were walking through a thick forest. They would have to come for them on foot. That suited Alice just fine. She, like most of the other survivors from the settlement had learnt to live off the land and to fight on foot, in the dark, and with nothing but the weapons they could carry. She had seen the awesome firepower Zeus could bring to bear, but also had seen that its troopers relied too much on air power and heavy weapons. Now they were on Alice's turf and she would make them pay for what they had done.

She asked the group to halt and scanned them. More than half were children too young to fight, or those who were too old or sick to fight against trained troopers. Everyone at the settlement knew how to handle weapons- after The Rising that was almost an elementary education every human child had to go through if they wanted to live beyond a few years. But it was one thing to snipe at mindless Biters and quite another thing to take on heavily armed and trained Zeus troopers. Alice picked a dozen young men and women, all of whom she had trained with and knew were good in close combat. She was the youngest of them, but nobody questioned her authority. Alice had always been acknowledged as someone with fighting skills well beyond her age, but with the role she had played in unearthing the deadly secret behind the Biters, there was even more of an aura surrounding her.

Alice asked the rest of the group to go ahead. She knew that there were some abandoned mines about five kilometers away and that was to be their resting place for the night. If they got there undetected, it would be virtually impossible for Zeus to locate them from the air, and once the Sun rose, she planned to make contact with the Queen. Her hope was that she would give refuge to Alice and her fellow humans. What followed then was something Alice had not had time to plan for or think through. Alice took the dozen she had asked to stay with her and asked them to gather in a circle.

'These are not Biters. They will not come in blindly to be shot. They have better weapons than us and they know how to use them.'

'Thanks for that inspirational speech, boss', one of the boys quipped.

Alice smiled as she replied.

'They are not Biters, but they are human, that means they will feel one thing Biters do not.'

'What's that, Alice?'

'Fear.'

~ * * * ~

Alice sat with bated breath, some thirty feet above the ground, hidden by the branches of the tree she was perched on. The others with her were similarly hidden, waiting for the Zeus troopers to appear. Two boys had been sent ahead as scouts, and when they had understood the likely route the troopers were taking through the forest, Alice had told everyone to take their positions. This was a tactic that they had often used before, born out of the simple insight that no matter how ferocious Biters could be, nobody had yet seen a Biter climb a tree. Alice could hear the troopers long before she saw their shadows in the dark.

'They move like pregnant cows', she thought to herself as she heard their heavy footfalls and their voices. For someone who had grown up in the open countryside, and learnt from an early age what it meant to move with stealth and in the darkness, Alice knew this form of warfare intimately. The Zeus troopers, used to swooping down from the air and with heavy air cover to back them up, found this totally alien to how they normally went to war. That was the fatal weakness Alice hoped to exploit.

As Alice sighted her rifle at the nearest shadow, a flicker of doubt crossed her mind. This was not like shooting Biters, whom she had regarded as lifeless, mindless zombies, but shooting men, men who would bleed, men who would scream and thrash about as they died, men who were perhaps conscripts in the Zeus force from other settlements. Then she remembered what she had witnessed at her settlement and steeled herself and opened fire.

A single shot rang out and a trooper fell, hit in the leg. He screamed aloud and his comrades stopped, watching for attackers they could not see. They had night vision optics on their scopes, but night vision was of use only when you knew what you were looking for. A flash bang grenade rolled towards the troopers and as it exploded, it blinded them, rendering their night vision useless and also illuminated them in a ghostly glow. Alice and her comrades opened fire, using carefully aimed single shots. The firing lasted for less than twenty seconds, and when it had finished, not one of the dozen Zeus troopers was standing. Alice whistled, and all of them clambered down the trees and ran towards their escape route. They would not go straight for the mines, lest they lead the troopers to the larger group headed there, but would create a diversion, moving North and then looping back when they were in the clear.

Alice ran through the trees, her heart hammering, and keenly aware of the sounds behind her. She heard several helicopters overhead, and while the helicopters would not be able to target them through the thick forest cover, it meant that Zeus had perhaps called for reinforcements. More troopers were coming after them to avenge their comrades and she thought she heard Appleseed bellowing orders. Part of her wanted to stop and seek her vengeance against him, but she knew that she would not be able to do what her father had entrusted her with by leading a suicide mission. With the element of surprise gone, they would be not much of a match for the more numerous and better equipped Zeus troopers. She had to regain the advantage of surprise otherwise they would not live to see the next morning.

It was impossible for her to account for every man and woman in her squad in the darkness and as she spotted a good hiding spot, she slid to a stop behind a large, fallen tree. She whistled, hoping her comrades would join her, and soon enough they were sliding into position next to her. She did a quick voice count and came up three short.

'Where are Rahul, Divya and Chetan?'

She was answered a second later when she heard

bursts of gunfire. A voice cried out for mercy and was silenced with a single shot. Alice blinked back tears and tried to think what to do. She knew how to fight, but had always counted on her father being there to lead everyone, to give direction. Now being accountable for the lives of so many was a responsibility she did not think she was ready for. But whether she was ready or not, she had to act because she could now hear the Zeus troopers coming closer.

'Everyone, let's move West over the irrigation canal and then we'll get to the mines.'

They moved instantly on her suggestion, running through the forest, their homemade and patched soft soles barely making a noise, in contrast to the heavy boots of the Zeus troopers now in hot pursuit behind them. Alice saw some shadows ahead of them and skidded to a stop as she saw one of them raise a rifle.

'Stop!'

Her warning was too late as a rifle barked and Alice saw the boy next to her fall. He screamed once and then was silent.

'They're in front of us!'

Alice had her group scatter for cover behind trees, but now she knew the awful truth. Zeus had not just been flying in reinforcements but they were using the mobility of their helicopters to flank Alice and her group. Now Alice had Zeus troopers on both sides of her, closing in on her position. She raised her rifle and fired at the nearest shadow, but could not be sure if she hit anything. The Zeus troopers, with their night vision scopes, had no such disadvantages. Two bullets slammed into the tree trunk inches from her face, showering her with splinters as she screamed and took cover, bleeding from her right cheek. Gunshots were ringing out all around her and now she had totally lost control of her situation. They were no longer a cohesive unit, but just eight or nine scared individuals in the dark against a larger number of heavily armed troopers.

She heard one of her friends scream in agony, and then something snapped inside Alice. Her life had been tough enough, but at least she had known a loving family, known the comfort that came from living among people who cared about each other. She was not going to have all of that taken away in one night because of the greed and cruelty of some men. She saw a large group of Zeus troopers emerge in front of her, and she took out her last remaining flash bang grenade and rolled it towards them, closing her eyes as it exploded, temporarily blinding the Zeus troopers.

She slung her rifle across her back and took her handgun in her right hand and her knife in her left and emerged from the shadows towards the Zeus troopers, running towards them at full tilt. The first trooper she encountered was one who was still rubbing his eyes to clear them. She fired two rounds, aiming for the face, knowing that the troopers wore body armor that would fend off small arms fire. As the trooper went down, she placed her right hand on his back, vaulting over him and coming up in a crouch as she brought her knife up into another trooper's leg. As he grabbed his leg and screamed, she stood up and fired into his face. Another trooper behind her was trying to raise his rifle when one of her friends shot him.

Alice jumped into the trees, leaving the disoriented Zeus troopers behind. She saw fleeing shadows and knew that she had bought enough time for her friends to get away, but now she was alone in the dark and surrounded by enemy troopers. She heard Appleseed shout.

'You little blond witch, come on out and I may still let you surrender. Don't make us hunt you down, because then it won't be pretty when we're finished with you.'

Alice tried to force herself to stay calm, but it felt

like her breathing was so loud that it could be heard across the entire forest. She pressed herself flat against a tree, and could hear Zeus troopers move all around her. It was just a matter of time before one of them looked in her direction through his night vision scope and the game would be up. She thought of climbing up the tree she was near but froze when she heard footsteps near her. There was a Zeus trooper on the other side of the tree, and she heard him unzip his trousers as he relieved himself. She stifled an urge to laugh at the absurdity of the whole situation, and waited till he moved on.

She peered around to see if the coast was clear and then moved slowly behind another tree. It was excruciatingly slow progress, moving from one tree to another, but at least she was moving closer to where her friends would be. The one thing she hoped was that they did not try and rescue her- that would be sure suicide with the odds against them. She stepped on a branch and the cracking noise made her cringe but when she heard no response from the troopers she moved on. And then she found herself face to face with a grinning trooper. The man was at least twice as broad as Alice and towered over her. In the dark, she saw the whites of his teeth as he grinned. It was the first time she got a close look at the troopers they were fighting and she realized that he looked very different from the brown skinned people of what had been known as India in the Old Days or even white-skinned people like herself. This trooper had narrow, slanted eyes and spoke with a strange accent. He must have been one of the Red Guards that people spoke of.

'Hello, darling. While the others get here maybe we could have some fun.'

As he reached out to grab her, his fatal mistake was that he saw a young girl alone in a forest, not a trained killer who had shot her first Biter when she was ten years old. Alice caught his wrist in a lock, snapping it back till she heard a popping noise, and as the man gasped in pain, she broke his nose with a back-handed strike with the thick ivory handle of her knife. She was tempted to shoot him, but that would have caused too much noise, so she stepped beyond the sputtering, sobbing man and went to the next tree.

That was when she felt a searing pain in her left shoulder and a split-second later heard the boom of a gunshot. Alice was lifted off the ground by the impact and fell hard against the tree, the wind totally knocked out of her. She felt for her left shoulder and her right palm came back covered with blood. She didn't know if it was a flesh wound or if the bullet had gone inside, but either way, she knew that unless she moved fast, she would lose too much blood and be too weak to continue. As she started to get up, a bullet smacked into the tree above her head and she flattened herself, feeling for the handgun at her belt. She pulled it out and readied herself, just hoping that she got a chance to take a few of the troopers with her.

She saw approaching shadows, wearing the unmistakable bulky body armor of Zeus troopers and carrying assault rifles. They were laughing and joking, no doubt thinking that they had killed her. Just then a large shadow leaped out from behind a tree and snapped the neck of one of the troopers. As the others turned to contend with their unseen attacker, two more shadows jumped on them and beat them to the ground, smashing their heads with their bare hands. The two remaining troopers turned to run, but the large shadow grabbed them and bashed their heads together, tossing them aside like rag dolls. As the three shadows walked closer, Alice got a better look at them. The large figure was the huge Biter who wore the floppy hat. He just stood there glaring at Alice and then slowly extended an arm with a grunt.

Alice took it, realizing that when all had seemed lost, help had come from the most unexpected quarter.

EIGHT

ALICE OPENED HER EYES AND barely able to speak with her parched throat, asked for water. Someone poured some cool water on her lips that she lapped up gratefully, and then lay her head down again, slipping once more into unconsciousness. She had no idea how long she had been out, and where she was, but the one thing she remembered were the dreams she had. Dreams of Appleseed burning her home, of strange slant-eyed men in black uniforms chasing her, and dreams of her father telling her that she must live.

When she finally awoke, she found her mother by her side. Her mother, always on the thin side, looked gaunt and haggard with her hair in a mess and cheeks that were stained with tears.

'Alice! Thank God you're ok.'

Alice managed to sit up and fell into her mother's arms.

'Mom, what happened?'

She learnt that she had passed out from blood loss from her wound, and had been carried back to the underground base where the Queen had led the survivors from the settlement. As she heard her mother's story, she learnt that the Queen had not abandoned them at all. Far from it, she may have saved all their lives. She had appeared in the forest and led the humans to an underground passage where they had been sheltering for the last three days, and had sent out some Biters to fetch Alice and any other survivors from the small band that had tried to hold off the Zeus troopers. Alice got up and walked around a bit with her mother's help and saw the large underground hall where all the humans were sheltered. They were huddled together in small groups and as Alice walked in, all of them stood up. They looked filthy, had not eaten a single decent meal or taken a bath in three days, but every single one of them smiled. Many held out their hands to shake hers when she passed and some of them hugged her. Alice's father may have appointed her to lead them, but her actions in the forest had earned her not just their leadership, but something more than that. She had earned their trust.

Alice looked towards the open door at the far end of the large hall and saw several Biters standing there. Bunny Ears was there, as was Hatter, and they all seemed to be just standing there, watching her. It was a curious dynamic- the humans knew that they owed their lives to the Biters and their Queen, and the Biters knew that Alice was somehow the key to their salvation, so they had to obey their Queen. Yet, both groups seemed to almost shrink from each other. Years of mutual hatred and fear could not be undone in a few days.

The Queen emerged from behind the Biters and watched as Alice made her way towards her. Now that her true self had been revealed to all the humans, she no longer bothered wearing her glasses or gloves, but stood there as she was. Just a few days ago, the humans would have considered it impossible to be in such a confined space with Biters without the two groups bent on mutual annihilation, but they had come to realize that the world was not quite what they had been taught to believe.

The Queen looked at Alice's bandaged wounds and then at her.

'I'm glad to see you have recovered. Thank you for the sacrifices you have all made.'

Alice suddenly remembered her father and the others who had been lost and struggled to keep her composure, leaning against her mother, looking more like a frail, lost young girl than the leader the humans took her to be.

'Alice, I know you have had a very tough time, but we do need to talk. Please come to my room as soon as you can.'

A few minutes later, Alice was in front of the Queen and the dilemma that was weighing on the Queen's mind was clear.

She could easily shelter more than a hundred humans in her underground lair, but she had no way of feeding them or getting them drinking water.

'We don't need any food or water, Alice, but you do. I cannot send my folks out to get it- they won't even understand what to get.'

Alice thought back to the years of scavenging, hunting, baking homemade bread, looking for wild fruits and berries and when they stayed in a place long enough, the occasional attempts at farming. With Zeus no doubt looking for them, there was no way such a large group could go out and look for food, so a smaller group would have to go out and forage for food and water. Alice immediately set about explaining the task, and after all they had been through together, she was not surprised when several dozen hands went up when she asked for four volunteers to scout the nearby area for food or water. She picked four of them, all young boys, all known to be fast and to have had at least some combat experience. She asked them to wait and went to the corner where her mother and sister were sitting to gather her weapons. Her mother held her hand tight.

'Alice, you must be crazy to head out in the state you're in! You've barely recovered.'

Alice looked at her mother, and gently removed her hand.

'Mom, I cannot ask any of them to head out if I'm not willing to go myself. Don't worry, I'll be careful.'

When they stepped out of the hidden entrance to the base, Alice saw that the Queen had chosen well. The entrance to the base was hidden among some old construction pipes. From even fifty meters away, nobody would guess what lay under the ground. Alice was carrying only her handgun and knife, and the boys with her were similarly armed. They planned to travel light, since the last thing they wanted to do was to get in a fight. They moved in the woods, and Alice kept her ears pricked, not just for any Zeus troopers but also for the sound of water. She knew that there was a stream nearby, and that was their best bet to get water. After just a few minutes of scouting, she heard something, and walked towards the source of the sound.

'Water!'

The boys were by her side in seconds, and they looked on with wide grins at the water flowing slowly in front of them. Three of the boys were carrying bottles tied around their waists and filled them one by one. It would hardly be enough for all the people with them, but it was a start, and Alice planned to get a larger group out to fetch more water once they knew the area was secure. Next they picked some of the nearby trees clean of berries and fruits and when they went back, they received a heroes' welcome. The meal they shared that night was frugal by any standards, but they were all smiling, and in their eyes Alice saw the glimmer of something she had though had been lost with the ashes of their settlement- hope.

So when the Queen came to visit them, Alice was understandably in good spirits. The Queen sat down in front of her.

'We cannot keep going like this forever. Now that Zeus and their masters are onto us, sooner or later they will crush us.'

Alice was a bit surprised at this frank admission of defeat.

'You were the one who wanted to fight them.'

The Queen looked at her with her lifeless, red eyes.

'Yes, but we cannot simply win in an armed conflict. That's why I so looked forward to you- a human who could help get our message and the vaccine into the right hands. They way I am, nobody would believe me.'

Alice's mother chipped in.

'You've seen what Zeus is capable of. Who could we possibly reach out to?'

'Mrs. Gladwell, of course I know many of the senior officers in Zeus are a part of the conspiracy, but do you really believe every foot soldier is? Most of them are not very different from what you were till a few days ago- scared humans from the Deadland who really believe the Biters are monsters out to exterminate them. Even at senior levels, there must be some people who also don't know the full truth. Such a conspiracy could not have involved everyone in the chain of command.'

As Alice went to sleep, she thought over the Queen's words. Was it really possible that there were men in power out there who were not part of the conspiracy? Was there hope after all?

~ * * * ~

A few days later, Alice and two others were on a scouting mission a few kilometers away from the base.

Alice was beginning to appreciate just how difficult and complicated managing logistics was. Feeding close to two hundred mouths required a lot of supplies, and they had to ensure that there were sources of food close by. She caught a glimpse of Hatter through the bush, and she knew the Queen had sent some of her Biters out to ensure that Zeus troopers were not nearby. There was still no real possibility of the humans and Biters co-operating in any organized way. The humans would likely listen to Alice if she told them that they were to work together with the Biters on their missions, but the Biters only seemed to take their orders from the Queen, and Alice did not want to risk them turning on the humans with them if they did get into a fight.

After a few minutes, Alice found a stream and asked the others to go back while she freshened up and followed them. She knelt by the water, and splashed the cool water on her face. She looked at her reflection in the water, and perhaps she was imagining it, but she looked different from what she had remembered. The old Alice always had a mischievous smile on her face, always looking to play jokes and pranks on the others in the settlement. A pixie, her father had once lovingly called her. The Alice that looked back at her had a harder face, with eyes that seemed more focused, yet much colder.

Alice got up to leave when she froze. She had just heard the voices of men talking nearby. She was in the open, with no cover and with no weapons on her other than her handgun and knife. If there was a Zeus patrol nearby, her chances of surviving a firefight were going to be slim. She flattened herself and crawled towards a gentle rise to her left and peeked over the other side. Sitting there, less than ten feet from her were three fully armed Zeus troopers. They apparently had not got wind of her, since they had their helmets off, with their rifles on the ground beside them, and were eating a snack. From their looks, Alice guessed they were local boys, which was confirmed when they began speaking to each other in a mixture of Hindi and English, a combination Alice had grown up both hearing and speaking every day. One of them, who looked to be the youngest of the lot, and perhaps not much older than Alice, seemed to be troubled by something.

'Ashok, you know what all the other guys are saying, don't you?'

The older and larger boy he had just spoken to spat on the ground.

'Jeevan, how many times do I have to tell you to keep both your ears and mouth shut? Don't you get it? We have a stable job. Our families get rations and are safe. Remember what our lives were like out in the Deadland?'

The third boy, who had stayed silent till now, looked up.

'Ashok, he does have a point. We signed up not just for the food and safety, but because we thought we would get a chance to protect other people and finally get back at the Biters who had taken so much from us. Where does the attack on a human settlement figure in that?'

Now they had Alice's full attention, since she realized that they must have been speaking about the attack on her settlement. Curious to know what else the troopers might know, she let her curiosity get the better of her and crept closer, peering as far beyond the edge of the rise as she dared.

'Naveen, they said they were traitors!'

The boy called Naveen whirled around at the older boy, his voice displaying barely controlled fury.

'Traitors? Why did our local officers not tell us anything about it before? Why was that explanation given after the attack by that bald white officer? And tell me this- why did they not use any local units for it, but flew in their Chinese Red Guards?'

It suddenly struck Alice why the troopers she had encountered looked so different from any men she had seen before. She had heard about China in the context of the Old Nations and about how the Red Guards were supposed to be the real army of the hidden masters behind Zeus, but she wondered why Zeus would fly in troops from there.

'Naveen, those troops were based in Ladakh, and you know the Red Guards are all Chinese.'

'It still doesn't add up, and I don't like it.'

There was an uncomfortable silence while the boys finished their snacks, and then began packing their kit. Alice began backing up the way she had come when she felt her foot hit something. She whirled around and saw a large Zeus trooper looming over her. She tried to reach the gun tucked into her belt, but he had his gun up in a second, and Alice found herself peering down the barrel of an assault rifle.

'Guys, we have ourselves some company!'

The other troopers clambered over the rise, and Alice was now surrounded by armed Zeus troopers. She got up to her feet and addressed the young trooper she had heard speak first.

'I heard you talk about the settlement that was attacked. I'm from there.'

The big trooper who had caught her spun her around.

'Talk to me! I'm in charge here, and you are my prisoner.'

He said the last word with a leer forming on his face, and in an instant Alice knew what his intentions were. A girl her age in more innocent times before the world had gone up in flames might have been paralyzed with fear in a situation like this, but for Alice, instinct and training came first, and fear followed only later. She kicked out at the boy's groin, making solid contact as the boy doubled over in agony.

Another boy tried to grab her from behind, but she caught his arm at the elbow, twisting it so he fell to his knees and then she kneed him hard in the face. The boy fell back, his nose broken as Alice jumped over the rise, sprinting for the cover of the trees. She heard guns being cocked behind her and prepared herself for the spray of automatic weapons fire that would no doubt follow when she heard an order bellowed with such force and authority that she found herself unconsciously slowing down and turning to see who it was.

'Hold your fire!'

She turned and saw Dewan standing there, with his rifle raised to his shoulders. For a second, she harbored hopes that he would rescue her but she realized that his rifle was pointing straight at her. Without taking his eyes off her, he spoke to the troopers.

'Do you morons ever think with your brains? Check the Communicator and see who she is.'

Alice was frozen in place, knowing that there was no way she could get away without being shot as one of the troopers took out a small device from his pocket and looked at it. All four troopers were now standing at attention in front of Dewan as he continued to give them a tongue lashing.

'She is a wanted terrorist not a plaything for you idiots, and I want her alive for questioning. Now go and join the unit and I'll bring her in myself.'

Suitably chastised, the four troopers left as Dewan walked towards Alice, his gun still raised.

'Colonel...'

'Shut up!'

Alice was shocked by the reply she got from Dewan, who had been so friendly and helpful when she had last met him. He kept his gun raised in his left hand while he took out a small device with his right hand and pointed it at Alice.

'Take a look at this.'

The screen showed a picture of Alice with a lot of words around it. On top were the words `Wanted'. Alice would have taken too long to try and decipher all the other words so she asked Dewan what it said.

'It says that you're a dangerous terrorist wanted in the deaths of several Red Guards and suspected of collaborating with elements who are out to destabilize the peace that the Central Committee is trying to bring to the Deadland.'

Alice almost laughed at the absurdity of it all.

'Come on, Colonel, you know I'm no terrorist. Do you even know what that Appleseed did?'

Dewan came close and now Alice could see that he looked frightened.

'I know it all, which is why I've been looking for you. I know this terrorist thing is all garbage, but I don't know why this is happening. When I found out what happened to your settlement and that they were hunting you, I came down to try and get to you first.'

Alice felt a wave of relief wash over her but she noticed that Dewan was suddenly alert.

'The rest of the squad will be here anytime. Got anywhere we can talk in private?'

Alice wondered if she should mention that her definition of private meant being in the company of two hundred people and several Biters, but thought better of it. She remembered what the Queen had said about finding someone in authority who would be willing to believe them, and Dewan seemed like her last hope.

She motioned for Dewan to follow her and they disappeared in the jungle before the first trooper got there.

~ * * * ~

Alice guided Dewan through one of the hidden

entrances to the base, which had been carved out of the trunk of a tree. Dewan looked around as he entered the narrow tunnel.

'How did you guys make such an elaborate hiding place in just a few days?'

Alice did not reply, weighing in her mind when and how she should break the full reality of her situation to Dewan. She needed him to be on her side and to trust her, and she was not sure if revealing the true nature of the Biters and Zeus would be too much, too soon. As they progressed down the tunnel far enough that Alice was confident they could not be heard overground, she asked Dewan to sit down.

'Colonel...'

'Just call me Amit.'

'Ok, Amit. There's a lot going on here that you need to know about. I don't know where to start, it all sounds crazy.'

Dewan laid a reassuring hand on her shoulder. He was very different from her father- he was shorter, built much broader and had a much squarer face but his eyes had the same kindness in them. Alice found it easy to be relaxed in his company as he spoke.

'Alice, I was a newly commissioned officer in the Indian Army. I had a girl I was going to propose to. I had a career to look ahead to. Then one day, my life and my world collapsed around me, and I found myself fighting for survival. I hid in the Deadland for months, surviving off the land, using my special forces training in a way I had never imagined before, fighting Biters and human scavengers alike, till I was picked up by a Zeus helicopter. They were the first promise of stability and safety in this crazy new world, and I signed up without a second thought. Since then, my life has had one purpose- to fight the monsters who had caused so much loss and to help the humans still in the Deadland. I never doubted anything I was doing, till now. So compared to what I have seen and been through, nothing you tell or show me can be too crazy for me to handle.'

Alice was about to begin when a shadow moved in front of her and she gasped. It was Bunny Ears, standing there looking at her, as if wondering why she was with a Zeus trooper inside the base.

'Holy Shit!'

Dewan was on his feet and was about to bring his rifle up. Bunny Ears, startled by the move, had bared his teeth and was hissing when Alice grabbed Dewan's hands.

'Amit, no! Please don't shoot!'

'But, this is...'

Alice looked at him, pleading with him.

'Just believe me for a minute and come further down. You'll see for yourself everything that I've discovered and the real reason behind why Appleseed suddenly wants me and my friends dead.'

Dewan seemed to be struggling with himself for some time. All his training and experience were telling him to open fire, yet he wanted to trust Alice. When Alice let go of his hands, she saw him look at her but then quickly shift his gaze to Bunny Ears.

'Alice, if you were a terrorist and you wanted me dead, I wouldn't be alive now. So I will trust you- but not this....thing. Any sudden move and I blow his head off.'

Bunny Ears growled as Dewan looked at him defiantly and an uneasy truce having been established between them, the three of them walked down the narrow path deeper into the base. When they entered the hall where the humans were sheltering, Alice heard several weapons being raised and cocked at the sight of a Zeus trooper in uniform. Alice stepped in front of Dewan.

'Please, he's a friend. He can help us.'

Everyone listened to Alice, but if looks could kill, Dewan would have been dead within a few paces with everyone in the room looking at him with undisguised hostility and contempt. Alice took him straight to the Queen's room, and apparently having heard of the arrival of a guest, she was dressed for the occasion, wearing her dark glasses and gloves and with a shawl covering her body. One glance at her and something clicked in Dewan's head and he took out his palmtop device.

'Let me guess. I am a wanted terrorist in your system, am I not?'

He looked sheepishly at the Queen who smiled, showing reddish teeth that caused Dewan to blanch as he began to wonder who or what he was dealing with. Alice asked him to sit and told the Queen about how he had helped her earlier, and then looked at Dewan.

'Amit, please listen to what she has to say and read the documents she has. That's all I ask of you- just listen to it all first before you say anything.'

Dewan sat impassively as the Queen took him through her tale, complete with all the documents she had and topped off with her revealing her true nature. Alice saw that Dewan didn't seem fazed at all by everything he saw. If anything, he seemed lost in thought, almost as if his mind were somewhere else. When the Queen finished, all eyes were on Dewan, waiting to see what his reaction would be. He got up and let his breath out in an audible sigh and then buried his face in his hands. Alice was worried that he was losing it and started to walk towards him, but he held out a palm, motioning for her to stop. When he finally spoke, it was in a tone that was barely a whisper.

'When people are scared enough, they begin to accept any form of tyranny because unquestioning obedience to unknown masters is better than facing known dangers.'

Alice sensed that Dewan needed to talk, so she stepped back as Dewan continued, talking more to himself than to anyone in the room.

'In all these years, I never asked who we served. All I heard was that the Central Committee had been set up in China and was overseeing all rehabilitation efforts, but I never asked who they were. I met my senior officers once in a while, and the only order they gave was simple- exterminate the Biters and bring more humans in the Deadland into settlements regulated by the Central Committee. When settlements refused to sign up, we were somehow assigned other duties, and we saw Red Guards from China who were flown in and kept in isolated camps on our bases, but we never asked why they had to come in.'

He stopped, and then looked at Alice, and she saw the beginnings of tears in his eyes.

'I saw thousands of people flown to China to be resettled. There were always rumors that they were being taken to slave camps, but I always ignored the stories, convincing myself that these were just conspiracy theories. You know the funny thing about everything you've shown me?'

Alice watched the Colonel come to grips with himself as he continued.

'The funny thing is that I and perhaps many other officers guessed that there was something going on, that this mysterious Central Committee was not just doing things out of the goodness of its heart, that we were serving masters whose agendas were not always transparent. But we had seen how chaotic and fickle life was in the Deadland, with no authority or government, and we chose to close our eyes and hang on to the illusion that we were fighting a just war. But what you've showed me goes so far beyond just today's reality- this could change everything!'

The Queen had been watching Dewan and now she came closer.

'Colonel, we need your help. We know we cannot survive a war against the Central Committee forever, but we need someone in the administration to help get the truth out. Is there someone in power we could reach out to?'

Dewan shook his head.

'I don't know and with Appleseed now so involved in the operations, I don't know whom to trust. As I said, I've never even seen anyone on the Central Committee, but you don't need to reach the top to get your message across.'

'What do you mean?'

Dewan looked at Alice as he answered her.

'We start at the bottom- with the common troops, young boys and girls from settlements like yours who form the backbone of Zeus here. That's where we get this thing started.'

NINE

SEVERAL OF THE HUMANS WERE gathered around Dewan as he dug into his backpack and took out a flat, sleek device.

'What it it?'

Alice's mother answered her.

'Looks a lot like a tablet computer, but I haven't seen one in years.'

Alice had grown up without many of the technological trappings and toys that kids had enjoyed before The Rising, and by the time she had grown up enough to understand what they were, the people at her settlement had lost or thrown away their computers and cellphones. She leaned over her mother's shoulder to see what Dewan had in his hand. The device suddenly seemed to come to life with bright, vivid colors appearing on its screen. She saw the Zeus logo, which was then replaced by lots of numbers and letters and symbols. As Dewan touched one of the pictures with a finger, a new set of visuals and text filled the surface. To Alice, it looked almost magical. Her mother was reading it aloud for the benefit of everyone around.

'The Central Committee has announced the

beginning of the new harvest season where workers are joyously participating in planting seeds and working the fields in preparation for a new year of prosperity. Chairman Wang has said that the Red Guards are vigorously pursuing heroic actions in the Deadland in India and America to continue their victorious charge against the Biter hordes and in helping bring more human survivors into the fold of the People's Revolution.'

Alice could see her mother's mouth twist in disgust as she looked at Dewan.

'What is this crap? Do the Chinese control everything now?'

Dewan looked at her, surprise on his face.

'Didn't you know? Oh I forgot, you guys have been off the grid for some time now. A few years after The Rising, when people started rebuilding, China was the only major power that was relatively untouched, and they set about taking charge under the Central Committee. They used the old Chinese Army as the beginning of the Red Guards but then contracted Zeus to help in the Deadland.'

The Queen was now right behind Dewan.

'I find it very convenient that the net outcome of The Rising was that the US and other powers were largely scattered and destroyed and China emerged as the centre of the new human civilization. I used to think that the US decision to hit China was madness on our part. Now, I'm not so sure. Perhaps it was true that the elites in the West who wanted a New World Order joined up with the Chinese to engineer this.'

Dewan sat in silence, considering it in his mind.

'Look, Dr. Protima, I was in the old Indian Army and we hardly saw China as a friend, but I'm not sure they would have done this. Why destroy the whole world and rule over the ashes?'

Alice's mother spoke up.

'Colonel, I worked in a bank in my old life, and we

all remember the way the world was. Markets were melting down and the US on the verge of defaulting on its debt. There were protests throughout the world against the elite who had brought the world to such a state. China's economy was booming but it was also the largest holder of US debt- if the US had collapsed and defaulted, China would have been ruined. Add to that growing demands for democracy in China, and the second Tinanmen Square massacre of 2012, and I don't find it hard to believe they could have engineered this. From what I see here- they seem to be fine, maybe because they prepared for it. They still have big cities, and are using slave labor from the Deadland to harvest their crops and feed their people. And every surviving human is so terrified that they are willing to live with any level of dictatorship if it means some level of safety.'

Alice's mind was reeling. Why would anyone destroy so much, and kill so many countless numbers of people to hold on to power? She began to understand why her father had hated men who craved power and had tried so hard to keep their settlement out of the clutches of Zeus and its masters. Now, as she looked at Dewan, she began to see the first cracks appear as he perhaps for the first time began to understand the role he had unwittingly played in the whole conspiracy.

Alice sat down next to him. 'Amit, what can we do to fight this army of theirs? Could you help train some of us or maybe help us get better weapons?'

Dewan shook his head.

'No, Alice. You cannot win this war through weapons alone. What you've seen is nothing compared to the firepower they have. The Zeus troopers only have personal weapons and some air support, but the Central Committee has missiles and heavy bombers. They would flatten us without us even getting a chance to take a shot at them.'

'So what do we do?'

Dewan was up and he began pacing the room.

'Exactly as I said before, we need to get the rank and file of the Zeus troops to know the truth. Once they know what they are doing and who they are really serving, we'll get more allies in the battle.'

Alice's mother was now holding the tablet and she looked at Dewan, an idea forming in her mind.

'We are totally cut from the information networks Zeus and the Central Committee uses, but you are plugged into it. If you leave this tablet here, we could post messages that all Zeus troopers would be able to see.'

Dewan clearly didn't think that was a good idea as shook his head vigorously.

'They would track the tablet down in a few minutes and how could...'

As he was saying something, he suddenly stopped, as if a new idea had struck him.

'What if I lost my backpack in a firefight and someone took my kit including my tablet?'

The Queen saw where Dewan was going and chipped in.

'Could any of us use this device? We haven't been near computers for years and this is more advanced than anything we used in our time.'

A man stepped forward.

'Hey, I was really into tech and was a blogger before The Rising. I'm sure I could learn if the Colonel here showed me the basics.'

'Then we have a plan.'

Alice looked at Dewan.

'Plan? We keep the tablet here, and figure out some way of getting messages to the Zeus troopers, but what about you?'

Dewan looked at her.

'I go back to my base, pretending to have survived a ferocious firefight and then continue being a loyal soldier to the Central Committee.'

Several people began to speak up at the same time, and the Queen had to raise her voice to hush them.

'Quiet everyone. Let him finish.'

'But how can we be sure he won't lead them here?'

Dewan turned to face the speaker, an elderly woman who shrank back under his gaze.

'Look, you just have to trust me. I took enough of a risk wandering out alone to look for Alice. If I just wanted to follow orders, I would have arrested or killed her when I had her alone in the forest.'

Alice heard a few more people grumble so she stood in front of Dewan and addressed the crowd.

'Everyone, on this you need to trust me. The Colonel didn't have to come down here with me; he didn't need to save me from his men in the forest and he certainly didn't need to put himself at so much risk by trusting me. I trust him, and ask you to go along with his plan if you trust me.'

Her words carried the day, and as Alice watched everyone back down, and many of the gathered people averted their gazes when she looked at them, she was once more surprised at what she had become. She had never wanted to be a leader of any sort, and certainly would not have asked for the responsibility and burden that came with it, but now whether she liked it or not, she realized that everyone was looking to her. She just hoped that she did not mess things up too much. Dewan touched her gently on the shoulder.

'Thanks, Alice. You'll all be better off having someone on the inside helping you.'

After brief goodbyes, Dewan gathered his weapon but left the rest of his kit behind and slipped out into the forest. He turned once to wave at her and then Alice saw him disappear behind the trees. Her heart was pounding as she wondered if she had done the right thing by letting him go or had doomed all of them.

~ * * * ~

Dewan was sitting at his desk, typing his After Action Report for the third time. He had sent in his first draft, which had been sent back by Appleseed with more than a dozen questions. He had tried to address all of them systematically, but knew that no matter what he wrote down in a formal memo, he could not address the underlying skepticism of how an elite officer like him was caught in close combat with terrorists and managed to escape without his kit. His second draft had gone through to the Central Committee in Shanghai and had come back with more notations and questions. Dewan had half-hoped that he would not attract too much scrutiny but with the high level of anxiety, even paranoia that Appleseed had about Alice and the escaped humans, he was not going to let Dewan off the hook so easily. Dewan noticed that Appleseed said nothing about the attack on the settlement and made no mention of the Queen. If Dewan had any doubts about what he had heard from Alice and the others, Appleseed's behavior nailed it for him.

The Messenger window on his screen beeped and he saw that he was being called for a debriefing to Appleseed's office. When he reached there a few minutes later, he was surprised to see Appleseed sitting with a Chinese General whom he had never met before. The slight man was wearing his cap even indoors, and as he stood, Dewan saw the red star emblazoned on his it. Dewan saluted and the man returned his salute.

'At ease, Colonel. I am General Chen from the Central Committee. I flew down from Shanghai last night to meet you for myself.'

Dewan was instantly on guard.

'Sir, I would have been available anytime for a call.

I'm sorry you had to travel so far on my account.'

Chen smiled, his thin lips pursed back, and Dewan realized that he was looking at a man who could be very dangerous.

'Colonel, you have had a number of brushes with the Biters recently, and you brought in this counter-revolutionary, this girl Alice. We have spoken to some of your men and it seems you had recaptured her when they last saw you.'

Dewan tried not to betray the fear he felt.

'Sir, I had her but when I was bringing her in, I was ambushed by a force of her supporters and I lost her.'

Chen looked at him for several seconds before turning his back to Dewan.

'Yes, Colonel, and it seems you lost much of your kit including your service tablet.'

'Yes, Sir. One of them grabbed my backpack and pulled it off.'

Chen was picking something off the desk and when he turned to face Dewan, he was carrying a tablet in his hand. He powered it on and tapped the Browser. When it opened up, Dewan saw a new post on the Intranet Board used by Zeus. His heart skipped a beat when he saw the headline.

What is the real truth behind The Rising? Read more to find out.

'Colonel, this was posted last evening. We triangulated the location to somewhere deep in the Deadland, but of course nobody was there when a squad got there.'

When Dewan replied truthfully that he had not seen the post, Chen smiled.

'Of course you did not. It was up for only five minutes before we removed it and locked your account from which it was posted. That won't stop whoever did it from creating new accounts and posting again, but it does make you wonder. Biters cannot use tablets, but their terrorist human collaborators can. Counter revolutionaries like this Alice of yours.'

The last two words caught Dewan totally off guard and he realized he was walking a razor's edge and that anything he said could land him in serious danger.

'Sir, I have devoted the last fourteen years to serving the cause we all fight for, and I want to help in any way I can.'

Chen dismissed him and told him that he could go and rejoin his unit.

'Colonel, I may take you up on that offer someday.'

Dewan reached his desk, his heart pounding. He knew his story was wafer thin, and the fact that Chen was here showed just how a serious a threat the Central Committee saw the situation as. Media and what had been recreated of the Internet was strictly regulated, and nobody had really complained, once again trading off democracy for security. But for the first time ever, that tightly controlled information flow had been breached.

A few minutes later, he went to the cafeteria to have dinner and saw several troopers there. He sat down next to a few young recruits and while they quickly shut up when he sat, he could see that they had been in the middle of an animated conversation.

'So guys, what were you talking about?'

One of the troopers looked around, as if seeking support from his comrades and then looked at Dewan.

'Sir, it's nothing, just some stupid rumors some of the guys had seen.'

Dewan had always been well liked by his men, not least because he was always accessible and was someone they could count on to help. Many of his men had been mere boys who had been picked up from the Deadland, and Dewan had trained them and in many cases, saved their lives in combat. He looked at a young trooper he knew well.

'Satish, what are these rumors?'

The young trooper seemed to be struggling with

how to say what was on his mind.

'Sir, it seems someone hacked into your account and posted some stuff about The Rising last night. A few of the guys happened to read it, and have been telling all sorts of wild stories.'

Dewan had to stop himself from smiling.

'I heard some bastards hacked my account. What did they post?'

Another trooper spoke, seemingly hesitant to even say the words out loud.

'Something about The Rising having been caused by human governments and about how China was behind so much of it.'

Another trooper, now more confident since the subject had been broached, spoke up.

'I also heard that it mentioned something about what all the folks from the Deadland were doing in the colonies being set up for them. Something about them being little more than slave labor. Sir, they may all be lies for all I know, but why would someone suddenly make up such lies and post them on our boards?'

He quickly shut up when a whole squad of Red Guards came into the cafeteria and sat at an adjoining table, and they continued their meal in silence but Dewan, despite the fear he had felt while meeting Chen, was exulting inside.

His plan was beginning to work. Now it was all up to Alice and her group to take it forward. With Chen and his Red Guards here in force, he knew they would hardly have it easy.

~ * * * ~

'Nikhil, hurry up!'

Alice was gnashing her teeth in frustration at the time Nikhil was taking to upload his latest post. She scarcely understood the technology involved in it all, but she knew that the Red Guards would know within minutes where the post had been uploaded from and would be sending troopers their way. So far, in the last week they had uploaded two posts. In both cases, they had ventured far from their base, making an overnight journey through the forests, uploaded the posts and then made their way back. Alice had no idea if anyone had even read the posts or what impact they were having, but Nikhil was sure that the Central Committee would be trying its best to delete or block the posts. Nikhil was over fifty and quite unlike most of the other men at the settlement. He was slightly built, and wore broken glasses that were crudely held together by adhesive tape. Before The Rising, he had claimed to be a blogger, though many of the older folks said he had been a hacker. Alice didn't really know what those words meant, but she knew that he was able to use the tablet Dewan had left behind and was willing to make the dangerous journey with her through the forest.

To minimize their chances of detection, only the two of them had ventured out. While that made for better stealth, it also meant that if they ran into trouble, their chances of survival were low. Alice was armed to the teeth, with her handgun, knife and an automatic weapon that they had salvaged from a Zeus trooper. But while Nikhil carried a handgun, she was not sure he even knew how to use it properly. To make things worse, he had been sitting hunched over the tablet for the last fifteen minutes, whispering something about firewalls. The post he was uploading was one that was a detailed first person account of Appleseed's role in the destruction of their settlement, based on Alice's story. It was a risk to personally identify her, but they had reasoned that putting a face to the messages would make it more believable than them being from anonymous posters. Also, with Alice supposedly a wanted terrorist, this would help sow doubts in the minds of Zeus troopers about who the real bad guys were.

Finally, he got up and looked at Alice with a look of triumph.

'It's done! And this time I waited to see if there were any responses so I could be sure somebody is reading our posts.'

Alice froze.

'You waited! You know they'll be coming soon. Let's get out of here.'

Nikhil persisted and handed her the tablet.

'Look at this.'

Knowing that this war was going to be fought and won as much with words as with bullets, Alice had finally got around to asking her mother to teach her to read and had been brushing up her reading skills. There was only one reply to Nikhil's post and it was short enough for it to not tax her reading skills much. A Zeus trooper had posted.

'So that's why the Red Guards are all over the place nowadays.'

Alice knew that whoever had replied to the post would likely get into a lot of trouble, but it was a small yet significant sign- their messages were getting through to the Zeus troopers and they were beginning to create some doubts in their minds. As Nikhil turned off the tablet and put it in his backpack, Alice heard the dull roar of approaching helicopters.

'Nikhil, come on! They'll be here any minute!'

The Sun had barely risen and Nikhil had timed his message to catch the attention of any Zeus trooper who was up but had some time to go before their morning drills. This was one among many details shared by Dewan which were helping them time their postings to coincide with downtimes for Zeus troopers when they were likely to be surfing on their tablets.

Alice and Nikhil were running into the trees when the first helicopter appeared over the horizon. Alice turned around and saw that there were two sleek gunships and a larger troop carrier. By the time the first Red Guards were on the ground, Alice and Nikhil were already more than a kilometer away, tearing through the forest as fast as they could run. From her previous run-in with the Red Guards, Alice knew that they would likely be trying to flank them and drive them into a trap, so instead of taking the path that led to the road which they needed to follow back to their base, they turned right, running through the forest till they came to a clearing. She could see the broken shells of old buildings. Nikhil had told her that once upon a time this had been a posh suburb and that some of the wooded areas they had run through had once been part of farmlands of the elite. That was a world that sounded totally alien to her, but she was happy for the cover the buildings would provide them. They ran into an old apartment building and rushed up the stairs. On the second floor, they stopped to see where their pursuers were, but saw no sign of them.

Alice relaxed a bit and took a look around her. For someone who had lived in the open for much of her life, it was hard to imagine living in these concrete shells, but then their occupants never had making an instant getaway as a priority. Perhaps if they had, they would have lived longer than they did during The Rising. The apartment was obviously abandoned and as they walked from one flat to another, they found little of use or interest, since they had been picked clean over the years. As Alice entered one flat, she saw something small lying in a corner. It was a small female figure with half burnt blonde hair.

'Nikhil, what is this?'

'Alice, that was a Barbie doll that girls used to play with.'

Alice flung the doll to one side, wondering how girls ever had enough spare time to sit and play with silly little figurines. She looked out the window and froze. There were a dozen or more Red Guards outside, their rifles at the ready, walking past the apartment. She motioned for Nikhil to get down as she continued watching the men outside. One of them was speaking into a handheld radio and as Alice looked up in the sky, she saw the faint outline of something black hovering above them. That must have been one of the drones Appleseed had mentioned, thought Alice, wondering if they had been spotted on their way into the apartment. Most of the Guards walked past and Alice was beginning to relax when one of them suddenly stopped and looked back at the apartment. Alice ducked down as he brought his rifle up to his shoulder, looked through the scope and casually fired a single round.

The bullet hit the wall just outside the window where Alice and Nikhil were sheltering, and they waited for a minute or more, hoping the Guard had moved on. Nikhil, tired of sitting on his haunches, started to get up to stretch when another bullet shattered the glass on the window. Nikhil dove to his right, and even without hearing the Red Guard's bellowed command to his men, Alice knew that the sudden movement had given them away. Alice was at the window in a split second, her rifle at the ready, and she fired at the first Red Guards approaching the apartment. Her bullets kicked up the dirt around them and she saw one of them fall before he was pulled behind cover by a comrade. Before she could find new targets, the other Guards opened fire on full automatic, shredding the window and showering her with glass. With the numbers so stacked against her, standing her ground and hoping to win the firefight was a losing cause.

She saw that Nikhil was crouched against the wall, and while his hands were gripping his gun, they were shaking uncontrollably. An idea came to her as she considered the odds against them.

'Nikhil, just point your gun out the window and fire

down at them. You don't even have to aim, just stick it out and shoot once every few seconds and please don't get yourself killed.'

He offered her a wan smile, as she took her rifle and ran out of the flat and down the stairs. She could hear the pop of Nikhil's gun, immediately answered by an overwhelming volley of automatic weapon fire from the Red Guards. She rounded the corner on the corridor and climbed out an open window that had once served as a fire exit. She crouched on the narrow stairwell outside and saw the Guards, four of whom were now advancing from cover to cover while their comrades kept up a withering rate of fire at the window where Nikhil was hiding. She was almost behind the Red Guards and they had not yet spotted her. She selected single shot mode, not wanting to waste bullets and aimed carefully at the Guards advancing on the apartment. Her first shot took a Guard in the neck, killing him instantly. Before the others had realized what had happened, another was down. By the time the Guards spotted her and their officer, a tall and thin man, screamed orders to his men, a third Guard was down.

As Alice dove back into the corridor, bullets slammed into the stairwell where she had been seconds ago. There were still nine Guards left and while she had managed to give them a nasty surprise, the odds were still very much against them. She retreated back up the stairs and found Nikhil grinning.

'Did I hit anyone?'

Despite all the stress, she smiled.

'Nikhil, you should stick to that tablet thing of yours.'

As she peered out another window, she saw that the Guards were again advancing on the apartment, and she brought her rifle up, determined not to go down without a fight. Just then, a dark figure wearing a hat rushed out from the forest and picked up the nearest Red Guard, snapping his neck and tossing his body away. Several more Biters jumped out of the bushes, and Alice saw the Red Guard officer shoot one in the head before beginning to run towards the apartment. Taken by surprise and outnumbered, the Red Guards never stood much of a chance, and two or three more were killed before Alice saw Hatter stand up to his full height and scream. The other Biters took his cue and the remaining Red Guards were not killed but bitten. The Officer who had been running towards the apartment raised his rifle, aiming straight at Hatter, who was now lunging towards him. The Red Guard Officer was about to pull the trigger when a single bullet from Alice hit him in the neck and he went down. Hatter looked up with his expressionless, red eyes and saw Alice at the window.

Alice had never been so happy to see Biters before and as she and Nikhil came down, they saw that the four Guards who had been bitten were now twitching on the ground, as if suffering a violent fit, and then they sat up, all trace of humanity gone in their lifeless eyes, blood from the bites they had suffered streaming down their bodies. They looked at Alice and Nikhil and one of them hissed and started to move towards them when Hatter hit him hard and then barked something to them. Alice didn't understand what he said, but it was clear that they knew who was in charge because as they ran into the forest to get back to their base, the newly converted Biters made no move to attack them. Alice turned back after a few minutes of running to see Hatter and the other Biters following them. Some distance behind them were the new converts.

Alice smiled and Nikhil asked her what she found so funny about their near brush with death.

'When the Colonel talked about us turning Zeus troopers to our side, I'm guessing he didn't have this in mind.'

TEN

'THREE HUNDRED?'

APPLESEED WITHERED IN the face of Chen's rhetorical questions. The one thing that Appleseed had learnt about his Chinese boss was that when he asked a question, he rarely wanted an answer. Instead, he was usually passing judgment, and in this case, Appleseed knew that the judgment being passed could be deadly for him. Appleseed had been a career military officer in the old US Army, when as a Colonel based in Afghanistan he had been approached by some old mentors who had mentioned certain special projects they wanted him to help with. At the time, a million dollars in cash seemed to be worth the secrecy and subterfuge he had dealt with, and when The Rising had taken place, he actually thought that he had been chosen to be one of the elites to fight this scourge. Fifteen years later, he was not so sure anymore about who or what cause he really served. The money was no longer worth much, but he did have a wife and three kids, and he knew that if Chen ordered it, in an instant he could be reduced to being no more than yet another of the millions of slave laborers who lived and died without much fanfare in the many camps that sustained the utopian new world that the Central Committee promised to usher in. The only currency he knew and recognized that still mattered in this new world was power, and he was determined to cling on to that.

He straightened his back and faced Chen, whom he towered over.

'Yes, Sir. Over the past one week, we have had more than three hundred desertions in the force.'

Appleseed saw Chen's pale face darken and his fists turn red as he clenched the chair in front on him.

'That, General, is the problem of using the occupied to manage their own territories.'

Appleseed bit his tongue. He knew how badly the Chinese Red Army had been hit by retaliatory strikes by US nuclear forces in the days following The Rising, and while the erstwhile United States was little better than the Asian Deadland Appleseed oversaw, there was continued fierce resistance from bands of American guerillas that was bleeding the Red Guards dry. He knew that Chen and his Chinese masters badly wanted to nip in the bud any possible insurrection in Asia and that they were counting on him to do it. That was the single most important source of Appleseed's power. For the past fifteen years, he had managed the Asian Deadland with an iron fist, born out of extensive experience in Afghanistan before The Rising, a fiery grounding in counter-insurgency that had helped him decimate the Biters and bring into the Central Committee's fold most of the remaining human settlements. That was of course till that silly girl called Alice surfaced and the whole matter threatened to spiral out of control. He felt a familiar stirring as he recalled being alone with her. In his mind, he was a soldier who was doing his duty, but there were dark moments and dark deeds that he tried hard to not consciously face, for in his hearts of hearts, he enjoyed the power he held over others, the power to make them submit to his will, the power to make them beg him. He recalled all the grief this Alice had caused him and promised himself that the next time she was alone with him, she would be begging him for mercy.

Over the past two weeks, her cohorts had been bombarding the Zeus Intranet with messages, averaging more than three a day, and while Chen had flown in Information Technology specialists from Shanghai who would delete every posting within minutes, the seditious messages were slowly but surely having an impact. The hardest hit were recruits from the human settlements in the Deadland of what had once been India, and desertions had been on the rise. All attempts to track down the posters had proven to be in vain and the efforts at striking back against them had produced little by way of tangible results other than many scores of casualties.

'Eighty-five Red Guards have died in one week. Does that sound like something the Central Committee will tolerate?'

Appleseed had posed a rhetorical question to Dewan not unlike the ones being posed to him by Chen, and he was infuriated to see Dewan standing impassively in front of him.

'Goddamit, Colonel! You've been patrolling these areas for years. Don't tell me you don't know where these people can be.'

Dewan looked Appleseed straight in the eye, and waited for a few seconds before replying, as if weighing how best to phrase his reply.

'Sir, General Chen insists on flying in Red Guards straight from Tibet or mainland China who know nothing of the local people or terrain. That's why they walk into one ambush after another. If they let me and my boys get a free reign, we may actually produce better results.'

Appleseed turned on Dewan with a fury.

'Colonel, the reason he does that is because he is not sure whether any of the local troops can be trusted. I hope I don't have to remind you of the number of desertions we've seen over the past couple of weeks.'

Dewan thought of how to reply to that, and when he did, Appleseed noticed that the Colonel was not looking him in the eye.

'General, the boys are no longer sure of what the truth is. These posters from the Deadland are sending out messages that challenge the very reason we are doing what we are. I haven't really seen the Central Committee counter those with any compelling arguments other than to censor the posts and send out Red Guards against locations where the posts were supposedly uploaded.'

'Colonel, I hope you realize that such statements about the Central Committee border on treason!'

Appleseed noticed that Dewan did not flinch under the implicit threat, and an idea came to him.

'Colonel, would you say that anyone not in approved settlements can be considered at the very least a sympathizer, if not an active collaborator with the counter-revolutionaries among the humans and no more deserving of mercy than the damned Biters?'

Dewan was taken aback by Appleseed lapsing into the lingo used by Chen and his Chinese masters and his hesitation led Appleseed to press ahead.

'I take it that this Alice and her cohorts could not move so freely in the Deadland if the remaining human settlements there did not at least implicitly support her?'

Dewan did not know where this was going and he knew that anything he said would not help his cause, so he just stayed silent as Appleseed continued.

'So, Colonel Dewan, from your response, I take it that anyone still in the Deadland in unauthorized settlements is probably a human sympathizer of this

Alice or have been subverted by the Biters and their supposed Queen. For years we have resisted taking active measures against the Biters in the Deadland because we wanted to minimize collateral damage among the human settlements there. Perhaps that equation has now changed.'

Dewan felt a chill go up his spine as he realized where this was going. Appleseed picked up his radio to call Chen.

'General Chen, I have a plan that may help us eradicate the threat we face once and for all'

As Dewan heard Appleseed outline his plan, he was seized with panic. He had to do something to warn Alice and the others, but there was no way he could do that without compromising himself.

~ * * * ~

'It's her!'

Over the last couple of weeks, Alice had slowly got used to this kind of reception whenever she walked into a human settlement in the Deadland. While Nikhil had kept up a relentless barrage of messages aimed at the Zeus troops, Alice had never really accounted for how fast the news would spread among the settlements. Most of the deserters found their way back to their settlements, and there they shared tales of the lies they had been told, of how the Central Committee, far from being a benevolent power, represented forces that had perhaps brought upon the catastrophe of The Rising in the first place to serve their pursuit of power. Most people found it hard to think of the Biters as anything other than the monsters they had always taken them for, but once doubts were sowed about the true nature of the Central Committee, they proved hard to undo. Add to that the heavy-handed tactics of the Red Guards and Chen, and one settlement after another had started to side with Alice.

Alice found herself facing more than three hundred people in the settlement, located just west of what had once been the suburb of Noida. Their leader, a grizzled old man, walked up to her and looked at her, as if sizing her up.

'You are but a young girl, little more than child, and a foreigner at that. What makes you expect that we would side with you and risk facing the Red Guards?'

Alice looked the old man in the eye.

'I don't expect you or your people to do anything other than to hear me out. After that, you can still choose to send your young ones to serve Zeus and to slave in the Central Committee's labor camps. Or you can choose to fight.'

The old man snorted derisively.

'Fight for what? You speak very fancy words for someone so young. Do you even know what those words mean?'

Alice did not even flinch as she replied.

'I fight for the freedom that we all have as human beings. The freedom to live the way we want, the freedom to choose our leaders, the freedom my father and hundreds of others have died to protect.'

The man averted his eyes and turned to the assembled crowd.

'Let us hear her out.'

When Alice finished, twenty more young men and women had joined her ranks. She never quite realized when her struggle to ensure safety and survival for her settlement had become something more. Perhaps it was when she watched her father and his friends be killed by the Red Guards, perhaps it was when she realized the full extent of the conspiracy behind it all, but what mattered now was that whether she liked it or not, she was effectively leading an ever growing army that fought back against the Red Guards. The

Biters still would not really take orders from her, but she noticed that they were always lurking in the background on the Queen's orders, waiting to wade into the battle to support her.

Alice waited on the small hill outside the settlement as Nikhil uploaded his latest message- about how more and more desertions were taking place. They had actually met a dozen deserters who had returned to their settlements and Nikhil had used the tablet's camera to record a few of their testimonies that he was also uploading. When he finished, he looked at Alice.

'I'm almost out of juice. We need to be heading back.'

Alice realized that the small tablet in Nikhil's hand had proved to be a more devastating weapon in their struggle than any amount of firepower, and she also understood that it needed recharging. Dewan had left a charger behind, but only one of the underground shelters had an old generator which was being carefully husbanded to provide limited electricity and now also to power up the tablet. Alice and Nikhil set off at a brisk pace, jogging more than walking through the forest. Along the way, Alice spotted three men with rifles who waved to her. Even if people had not met her, almost everyone seemed to know about the blond haired girl who was fighting back. As Alice ran faster and faster, she felt Nikhil fall behind, but she wasn't worried. There was no sign of Red Guards nearby and they had only about five kilometers to go before they could disappear underground. Running always helped clear her mind, and Alice realized just what a motley crew she was leading. There were of course the people from her own settlement, who she knew would follow her to the end, then there were some from other settlements in the Deadland who had supported her but would not trust the Biters and so chose to stay in their own settlements while helping her with scouting, and finally there were those who said they wanted to help but would not bring themselves to follow a young girl, and remained uneasy allies at best. Even among the Biters, Alice had realized that while the Queen commanded the loyalty of many of them, there were small bands in the Deadland who had gone almost rabid, crazed with fear and hate, and would attack any human on sight. That made it tougher for her to sell her story of how the Biters could be worked with. It was all such a complicated mess that it made her head hurt and made her wish that she did not have to be the one to deal with it all.

'Alice, stop!'

Alice slowed down and saw Nikhil bent over, holding his knees, trying to catch his breath.

'Nikhil, the Red Guards will be at the site of our last transmission any time. We need to get underground as soon as we can.'

Nikhil closed his palms together, in a theatrical show of begging for mercy. Alice laughed out loud. Nikhil was not much of a fighter, but he was fun to have around, and he was the only one who knew how to use the tablet and that made him invaluable.

'Ok, get a drink of water and we'll be on our way.'

Nikhil took out a bottle from his backpack and drank and when he was about to put it back, took out his tablet for one last look.

'Let me see if they've already taken down my message.'

Alice watched his expression and knew that something was very wrong.

'Nikhil, what happened?'

He called her closer and showed her the screen. There was a single message.

'To all friends in the Deadland- keep you heads down. Heavy downpour expected soon.'

The message had been uploaded from Dewan's account. Alice ground her teeth in anger and frustration.

'Why the Hell would he expose himself by posting like that? Appleseed and the others will be sure to question him.'

Nikhil turned the tablet off.

'Alice, he was trying to be as cryptic as he could, and I guess he could claim it was aimed at his men and comrades on mission in the Deadland, but he would take such a risk only if he desperately needed to get a message through to us.'

'What...'

Alice never got a chance to finish her sentence as her voice was drowned out by the drone of multiple jet engines overhead. Alice looked up see dozens of jets approaching from over the horizon. She had seen the occasional Zeus attack helicopter, but she had never seen aircraft such as this- large bombers with swept wings, flying in formation, darkening the sky like a swarm of locusts.

'Nikhil! Are they coming to bomb where we last transmitted from?'

She saw that Nikhil was staring at the approaching armada, his face frozen in fear.

'Alice, they don't need so many heavy bombers to target one location. That fleet could flatten many, many miles of land.'

'Could they get through to our underground shelters?'

Nikhil never took his eyes off the approaching aircraft as he replied.

'I don't know. Some of them seem to be hardened bomb shelters that were built before The Rising, but the rest are no more than old sewers, maintenance tunnels and underground parking lots. Those wouldn't survive a direct hit. And nobody in the open would have a chance.'

Alice thought of the hundreds of people including her mother and sister in one of those shelters and of the hundreds, perhaps thousands of human settlements overground in the Deadland.'

'Nikhil, we've got to...'

Alice stopped in mid-sentence. She really didn't know what she could say that would be even remotely adequate. They couldn't really warn anyone, and there was no question of saving anyone else's lives. They were still more than a kilometer away from the underground entrance that would lead them to where the rest of their group was hidden. She stood quietly for a minute, looking back at the direction they had come from, and she could see several pillars of smoke rising in the horizon. Fires at the human settlements, where people were seeking warmth or perhaps cooking their frugal meals, and perhaps like Alice and Nikhil, watching the approaching fleet, not knowing what was coming their way.

Alice felt Nikhil pull hard at her arm.

'Alice, they aren't that far away. All we can do is run and try and find some cover.'

Alice ran like she had never run before and soon they could see the three large yellow leaves laid across a branch that signaled the entrance to their underground passage. Alice turned to say something to Nikhil, and saw that he was struggling to keep up. She screamed something to him, but her voice was now drowned out by the roar of the dozens of engines overhead. Alice dove through the branches and clambered on all fours through the narrow passageway, hoping that Nikhil was following. She knew that there was little cover overhead other than tree trunks and kept going faster, her palms and knees cut and scratched in a dozen places as she reached the near vertical drop that led to the hardened bomb shelter below. She dove in as the first bombs hit and she fell to the concrete floor. As she managed to sit up and get her bearings she felt the ground shake all around her and bits and pieces of the concrete roof chip off and fall as the bombs continued to rain down.

There was no sign of Nikhil. She screamed out for him several times but heard no response. In the darkness, she felt along the walls for the unlit torch she knew would be there, and from her backpack took out the small can of fuel and flint she needed to light it. When it was lit, she saw that larger pieces of the ceiling were now falling down towards her and when one particularly large piece missed her head by inches, she hung the torch on the wall and lay down in a fetal position, with her head covered in her hands. The rumbling continued and she thought she heard a voice and she looked up to see Nikhil at the edge of the drop. He threw his backpack down and was about to jump down when there was a huge crash that lifted Alice cleanly off the ground and threw her across the corridor.

Then she saw no more.

~ * * * ~

Dewan studied the pistol in his hands, wondering just how much easier it was to take another life than to contemplate taking one's own. He had no family and not much that he could say he had to live for, yet it seemed awfully hard to put the gun to his head and pull the trigger. He had shot others, men and Biters, dozens of times without conscious thought in the years of fighting that had dominated his life, but now he could not bring himself to do the same to himself. It wasn't just fear that held him back, though that was certainly there, but a feeling of infinite sadness that came from realizing that his life had not really amounted to much after all. He had spent most of his life serving a cause that had been a lie, and when he thought he had a chance to make amends, it was all too little, too late. He had seen the heavy bombers fly in from Tibet and knew that Chen's orders were as simple as they were brutal. He had ordered a saturation fire-bombing of the Deadland near Delhi, with wave upon wave of flights till nothing remained. Dewan had been unable to face his own troops in the cafeteria, local boys who had looked at him with horrified eyes. He had no answers for the questions behind those eyes. No answers as to why their friends and families had just been sentenced to a horrific death by the same Central Committee they were serving to supposedly help human survivors.

Hundreds of Red Guards had flown in the night before and all Zeus units where desertions had taken place had been disarmed and were now effectively under arrest. The Central Committee propaganda machine was in overdrive with reports about how counter-revolutionaries and terrorists had subverted some isolated units in the Deadland in North India and were currently being pacified by the heroic efforts of the Red Guards. Dewan had taken the risk of sending out his warning, but he knew it was likely to be too late. He also knew that it was too late for him. The Red Guards would be coming for him soon. As he put the gun to his head one last time, he heard footsteps outside his door and he paused. No, if he was going to die, he would at least put what remained of his life to some use after all.

He brought up the browser on his tablet and logged in to his official email account. He had already barricaded his door with a bulky bookshelf and he heard banging on the door as he began typing. He wrote at breakneck speed, writing of what he had learnt, of the deception behind The Rising and then of how Chen and his masters in the Central Committee were misleading all Zeus troops. He heard shots as the Red Guards outside shredded the door with automatic weapons and began kicking it open. Dewan finished and pressed `send' as the first Red Guard came in. Dewan flung his tablet at the man and as the Red Guard lost his balance, shot him twice. Two more Red

Guards came into the room and Dewan put them down with single shots to the head. Years of hunting Biters had taught him a thing or two that were finally going to be put to some use, he thought as he picked up the first Guard's rifle and rolled behind his study desk. He saw feet gathered outside his door and fired a short burst, hearing screams as the Guards took cover. He heard something hit the floor and looked to see a black cylinder rolling towards him. As the stun grenade went off, he closed his eyes, but he had not been fast enough. When he opened his eyes, he saw little more than flashes of white and black and he stood up unsteadily, trying to gauge from the footsteps where the Guards were and fired his rifle on full automatic, not knowing if he hit anyone. He was trying to blink away the bright lights when the first bullets struck him.

Alice opened her eyes, and the first thing she felt was the wetness on her face. For a moment she wondered where all the water had come from but the rusty smell and the acrid taste told her that it was her own blood. She got up gingerly, and as she looked around she saw that the passageway she was in was bathed in light. She looked up to see a hole in the ground above that had been blasted open by the bombing. Several large pieces of concrete lay around her and as she felt the throbbing lump on her head from which blood still flowed and the countless scrapes and cuts all over her body, she knew that she had been hit by her fair share or more of the debris. Still, she was alive, and that was something to be thankful for. She took a deep breath and felt her ribs hurt, and hoped that she had not broken anything inside. The dust raised by the shattered concrete made her gag with every breath and she found that the passageway leading onto the tunnels she had planned to enter had collapsed. She tried to grab handholds on the walls to climb out of the hole caused by the bombing and then she saw Nikhil. Or rather, she saw his hand, still grabbing his tablet. The rest of him was hidden under a giant slab of concrete. Alice knelt down beside him for a few seconds, feeling his lifeless, cold hands and then she took the tablet from his backpack, putting it into hers.

'Goodbye, Nikhil.'

She climbed out and saw something that looked like the Hell that the old religions had believed in. Some humans still prayed before their idols and crosses and holy books, but Alice had never really been brought up with any particular gods to believe in. Her father had once told her that there must be a power beyond human comprehension, otherwise The Rising could never be explained, yet it was vain and stupid to create our own vision of these gods and fight over whose vision was right. The fear of Biters and human marauders hunting you down had a good way of making people band together, irrespective of the gods they once worshipped. Nevertheless, Alice now knew what the old religions had meant when they spoke of a place called Hell. All around her, the forests were on fire, vast charred swathes of ashes and burning stumps that finally did justice to the name this area had carried for years- the Deadland.

Alice ran as fast as she could, desperate to reach her mother, sister and the others. After a few minutes of running, she came upon the ruins of a small settlement. The dozen or so small tents had been almost vaporized by the bombing, and other than ashes and a few scattered limbs, there was no sign of any people. Alice gagged and threw up on the ground, blinking back tears.

How many thousands had died today? What kind of men could be capable of such evil?

The answer was right there for her to see. The same kind of men who had almost wiped out human civilization so that they could rule over the ashes. The same men who now hid behind the anonymity of the Central Committee and used the Red Guards and Zeus troopers to enforce their will, wiping out any remaining trace of resistance and ruling over their empire while the rest of humanity lived and died like animals.

Alice ran on, her mind plagued with worries for what had happened to the others but through the agony she felt in her mind and body, one thought was crystal clear.

She would make sure Nikhil and the thousands of others who had perished today would not go unavenged.

ELEVEN

ALICE RAN THROUGH A CHARRED forest, trying hard to see through the smoke and to breathe despite the suffocating fumes all around her. Much of the ground was still burning as far as she could see. What kind of weapons had the Red Guards unleashed that had caused such damage- turning acres of land into a sea of fire? She raised her hands to her mouth, trying to stifle a gasp of horror as she saw a gaping hole where the entrance to their shelter should have been. She kept hoping that perhaps people would have had a chance to go deeper into the hardened shelters further underground, but as she ran closer she knew she was hoping against hope. People would have stayed in the larger but less secure chambers close to the surface. There was no reason for them to cram into the smaller chambers deeper underground as they had no warning of what was coming. She stopped abruptly as she saw what the hole in the ground revealed, and then she fell to her knees, crying and screaming as she saw dozens of bodies heaped upon each other, many burnt beyond recognition.

Alice didn't know how long she just sat there, afraid to go in and see the true extent of the horror inside and unwilling to confront her loss. She felt a hand on her shoulder and whirled around, ready to fight. Instead she saw the Queen standing there unsteadily, her body cut in dozens of places and her left hand a stump below the elbow.

'Alice, it's all gone. They are all gone.'

'Mom...'

The Queen shuffled away, mumbling to herself.

'All gone. All gone.'

Alice jumped into the hole, and thirty minutes later was back, sitting with her back against a tree, her mind vacant with the loss and the horror she had just endured. There had not been a single human survivor, and from what she could see, all the Biters inside had also been incinerated. She took the pistol from her belt and toyed with it. A single pull of the trigger was all it would take, and she could end it all. What was the point of a life where she had lost every single person and thing she had taken to be her own in just a few days?

She felt someone standing next to her, and she looked up to see the Queen there. There was no emotion on her face, but she seemed to be looking into the distance as she asked Alice to put the gun away.

'Alice, the prophecy still lives.'

Alice saw that she was holding onto the book she treasured so much in her remaining hand. Alice grabbed the charred book and threw it away, turning on the Queen with a fury.

'Damn you and damn your stupid prophecy! Look around us- everything's gone. Everything!'

Alice walked away and sat down against a tree, sobbing. From the corner of her eyes, she saw the Queen get up and walk towards the book. She picked it up and then Alice saw her expression change as her lips curled back, revealing her jagged teeth and like a cornered, wild animal she hissed and spat at someone approaching from Alice's right. Alice looked up and saw more than a dozen fully armed Zeus troopers standing there, automatic weapons in their hands. Instinctively Alice felt for the gun at her belt and even before her hand reached the gun, she knew that she would never have enough time.

A young trooper stepped ahead of the others.

'You must be Alice.'

Alice still had her hand on the gun, weighing in her mind whether she should just try and take at least one of the Zeus troopers with her instead of being taken alive. The trooper must have sensed what was on her mind so he put his rifle on the ground.

'Relax. We're not here to kill you or arrest you.'

Alice kept her hand on the gun but now took a closer look at the troopers. They looked like they had just come out of a battle- many had cuts and scrapes from running through the forest, and at least one had a bloody bandage around his head. The trooper extended a hand, and as Alice got a closer look at him, she saw that he must have been very young, and looked like a local boy, certainly not one of the dreaded Red Guards.

'Alice, my name is Satish. I was from a settlement near the old city of Agra. All of us were drafted into Zeus from settlements in the Deadland.'

He turned to see the Queen, who was still on edge and Alice could see his eyes widen but he made no threatening move.

'Dr. Protima, I presume.'

The Queen stopped hissing, but still stood rigidly, her book clutched to her chest with her one remaining arm.

'Satish, how do you know who we are?'

The trooper smiled.

'A blond girl and a half-Biter are not exactly a common sight in these parts. Plus, Colonel Dewan had given all the details of who you were and what role you'd played so far.'

At the mention of Dewan's name, Alice sat bolt upright.

'The Colonel. Amit. Is he okay?'

Satish motioned for the other troopers to fan out.

'Guys, keep a watch while I fill them in on what's going on.'

He sat down in front of Alice and took out a tablet from his backpack. Alice saw that the Queen, while not feeling at ease enough to join them, had come closer to listen to what he had to say.

He told them about how initially Dewan had pretended that someone had just hacked into his account to post the first messages, and then when messages started being posted from other accounts created by Nikhil, he never showed any signs of support in public. However, when the Red Guards were brought into the Deadland in ever increasing numbers and their tactics kept getting increasingly brutal, his men had sensed a shift in his mood. When troopers began deserting, he stayed at his post, but on more than one occasion, he saw troopers slip out but didn't raise the alarm.

'But none of us knew just how deeply he supported your cause till in his last moments, he posted this. We all saw his last warning when he learnt of the air raids, but it was all too late to warn anyone in the Deadland. The Reds have deleted his post, but I saved a copy to my tablet.'

Satish held his tablet up and both Alice and the Queen skimmed it. Dewan had laid out everything he had learnt. Coming from anonymous posters, such messages could always have been dismissed and countered by official propaganda. Coming from a veteran officer in Zeus, it would have been explosive, and with the devastation the air raids had unleashed on the Deadland, there was now more or less open mutiny among the local Zeus troopers.

'Is that why you deserted? What happened to the

Colonel?'

Satish looked at Alice and she noticed that he was quite terrified.

'Red Guards were hunting down all local troopers. We managed to get out just in time to save our lives. I'm not sure if the Colonel made it, but I heard that they sent several units to attack his quarters.'

Alice looked at the Queen.

'They've now declared war on their own troopers! That's crazy. Why would they do that?'

The Queen was studying the tablet as she replied.

'Alice, troopers like Satish have always been expendable. If what Dewan wrote about the ongoing insurgencies in other parts of the world like America is true, then using local troopers under Zeus just helped them wipe out the remaining Biters and ensure human settlements continued to provide labor while their main forces were being used to suppress resistance in what was the United States.'

Alice was looking off into the distance and the Queen asked what was on her mind.

'I'm thinking of how we could fight this war.'

~ * * * ~

The next week went by in a blur. Alice, the Queen and the Zeus troopers spent much of it in hiding from the Red Guards who had been airdropped across the Deadland to mop up any survivors. With much of the foliage burnt out and a lot of the underground passages and tunnels exposed by the bombing, they were forced to use a different tactic, and instead of moving deeper into the Deadland, they moved into the heart of what had once been the city of Delhi. There they sought refuge among the ruins of the buildings that had once been the landmarks of the Indian capital. Almost all the buildings bore signs of damage, the result of the many waves of devastation Delhi, like many other cities had suffered. The ravages of The Rising, the nuclear bursts that came soon after, and then years of warfare that had followed till the remaining human survivors had left the city to seek refuge in the Deadland had all taken their toll on the city. Now what had once been the bustling, overcrowded city of Delhi looked deserted, but Alice knew better than that. The Queen had told her that several bands of Biters were likely hidden in the city, usually emerging at night.

Alice saw a tall building which had half of its top cleaved off, as if a giant unseen hand had taken an axe and chopped it off. The Queen muttered.

'Well, I guess we'll have 5 Star accommodation tonight. Welcome to what's left of the Taj Hotel.'

Satish, as young and inexperienced as he was, had become the de facto leader of the Zeus troopers and he told three of them to take up positions near the lobby to watch for any attackers while the others went deeper into the hotel. Alice had never been in a hotel before, though she had heard stories of the nice hotels her parents had been to when they had gone on holidays before The Rising. Imagine that! Someone to bring you food and drink whenever you wanted and a warm, cosy bed to sleep in instead of a dirty old sleeping bag. Alice wanted to go upstairs and look at the rooms but Satish stopped her.

'The stairs looks pretty unstable and I don't want us to be stuck in here if there's any trouble.'

So they lay down in what had once been the lobby and Alice was about to sleep when one of the sentries spoke in a hoarse whisper.

'Folks, I see multiple shadows approaching!'

All around her, Alice heard the sounds of guns being loaded and cocked. She had only her pistol with her, having lost her rifle in the bombing, but she quickly rushed to a window to see what was happening. As she looked around her in the darkness, she realized that the Zeus troopers may have been lavishly equipped, with their night vision scopes and rifles, but most of these boys had never seen much combat before. Satish was hurrying to get them into position and she saw them fumble their way in the dark. With an army like this, Alice realized their war was off to a pretty bad start.

Satish crawled up next to her, and she saw that he was carrying a spare assault rifle, which he handed to her with a smile.

'I think you can use this better than most of these kids.'

Alice took the rifle in her hands and flipped on the scope and looked through it. In the ghostly green light of the night vision scope, she saw a large mob appearing over the driveway that led to the hotel lobby. She switched off the scope, knowing that they needed to preserve the precious batteries of the night vision sights till they found refuge someplace with a generator which they could jury-rig to recharge them. What she had just seen did not make any sense. The figures were not moving like Biters, but like humans. However, there was no way such a large group of Red Guards would just amble up to them in the open, where they were sitting ducks for the defenders.

'What do you make of it? Should we fire?'

Alice shook her head.

'No, Satish. I don't think they mean to attack us. They probably outnumber us three to one or more, but walking in the open like that means we could pick them all off with probably little or no losses. I think they're trying to signal that they're friendly.'

'Friendly? Who could they be?'

As if by way of reply, a male voice spoke up outside.

'Which one of you is Alice?'

Satish was about to rest a restraining hand on Alice's arm, but she replied.

'Who is asking?'

'Why does that matter?'

Alice sighted her rifle on the man who had been speaking and saw him through her night vision scope. He was heavily bearded, wearing a cap and carrying at least two rifles slung across his back, but his hands were held up in front of him. She spoke up again.

'It matters because it determines whether I greet you with a smile or a bullet through that silly cap of yours.'

She heard several chuckles outside and the man answered, his voice now much softer.

'We are friends. We come to join you.'

Satish and the troopers covered her while Alice stepped out. She still had her rifle at her shoulder but she lowered it when she saw the man smile and motion for all those with him to put their weapons down on the ground. There must have been over thirty of them, men, women and some children. Every one of them was carrying at least two guns, which Alice noted seemed to be all weapons taken from Zeus troopers or Red Guards. The man stepped forward, extending a hand that Alice shook.

'Alice, we have heard so much about you. My name is Arjun and we would like to join your group.'

For a minute Alice was too surprised to reply. She had never really consciously thought that she was leading anyone or anything. They had just been so focused on staying alive for the last few days that she had not had much time to think of anything beyond immediate survival. Arjun coughed softly, which snapped her back to reality. To her surprise, he seemed to be almost pleading.

'Look, we may not seem like much, but we can all fight. Give us a chance.'

They all walked in and sat around the lobby, with the newcomers looking at the armed Zeus troopers with some initial suspicion. Satish broke the ice by offering his hand to Arjun.

'Arjun, we're all local boys and all on the same team. We've been trying to escape the Red Guards for the last one week and finally decided the Ruins may be a better bet than the Deadland, or what's left of it.'

Arjun sighed and sat back.

'I know, we've been tracking you since you entered the Ruins.'

Alice spoke up, the surprise in her voice evident.

'Tracking us? But we...'

Arjun smiled, his eyes creased with years of worry, and making him look much older than his forty years.

'When The Rising happened, we decided to stay and protect our homes instead of escaping out of the city as many did. The first few years we lived like rats, then we began to fight back- against human looters and the Biters alike. You never saw us, but we saw you.'

He turned to Satish.

'Zeus never came in here much. It's easier to pick off targets from the air but that's of no use in a built up area like this. We'd meet and trade with folks in the Deadland but when we learnt how Zeus was taking over, we decided to stay here and remain free.'

Alice had always taken for granted that only Biters remained in the ruins of the old city, but as she was learning, there was much more to the world than she had ever imagined. She asked the question that had been on her mind ever since Arjun's group had shown up.

'How did you know about me?'

Now it was Arjun's turn to be surprised.

'Everyone knows about you! Many more troopers like Satish and his friends have been through the Deadland and the Ruins. They all have stories from what they read and heard, and some of them passed these papers out. Word spreads fast. We all lost everything in The Rising, and now that we know who was behind all the misery we faced, we want to help fight back.'

Alice saw the paper in Arjun's hand and saw that it had Dewan's last email printed on it. Even in death, the Colonel had more than done his duty.

***

'It's going to blow!'

Alice hid her head in her hands as the Improvised Explosive Device went off with an ear-splitting boom. When she peered back around the corner, she saw the results of the first ever IED she had rigged. Half of the target building was blown off and smoke and dust covered the whole area.

'Amazing what you can accomplish with a humble gas cylinder, isn't it?'

She turned to see Arjun standing there, grinning. Over the last two weeks, more human survivors in the Ruins had sought them out as well as close to a hundred more Zeus deserters. While Alice had naively believed they would all stay together, Arjun had told her to scatter them across the Ruins, to be kept in touch via a system of messengers. Satish and the other Zeus troopers were heavily armed, and Alice was skilled well beyond her years when it came to combat, but when it came to fighting in a congested, built-up environment like the Ruins, Arjun was the resident expert. His people called him General, but he had once sheepishly admitted to Alice that he had no military experience, but had been a salesman before The Rising. When he lost his young family in the chaos, he fought to survive and there his mastery of his former sales routes served him well.

With more than three hundred people now in her force, Alice had asked aloud how they should plan their campaign. Bitter at all she had lost, she had been tempted to lash out, but Satish and Arjun had convinced her otherwise.

'Alice, the Red Guards will smash us if we

challenge them in the open. We need to lure them into the Ruins and bleed them.'

The Queen had been quiet and withdrawn for much of this time, and Alice wondered if it were because she had been so used to being among Biters that she found it hard to adjust to human company. That night, the Queen came to Alice as she was about to go to sleep.

'Alice, I want you to keep something.'

She thrust the red vial that contained the vaccine into Alice's palms. When Alice protested, the Queen insisted she keep it.

'Alice, I had foolishly thought that we could find some honest men in power who would help us. It looks like we are condemned to a life of war now, but I don't want to give up hope. Keep it with you and if there is someone we can trust, hand it over.'

Alice woke the next morning to find the Queen gone. Nobody had seen her slip out during the night, and when Alice mentioned it to Arjun, his face darkened.

'Are you sure you can trust her?'

Alice was shocked at his reaction. She had been genuinely worried about the Queen being on her own in the Ruins.

'Alice, there are still bands of Biters in the Ruins, and there are areas we never go into. She seemed sane enough and I know that she and her followers helped you but the Biters in the Ruins are crazed and would rip our throats out any chance they got.'

'She is not going to betray us.'

Alice said those words and walked away, hoping that her faith in the Queen was well placed. They did not get much of a chance to talk about it further because they soon got busy in planning their first operation.

As Alice watched the men and women move about their drills, she saw just how far they had come. Now it was impossible to tell apart someone who had been a Zeus trooper living in the relative luxury of their barracks and someone who had spent years hiding and fighting as a `Ruins Rat', as they had come to be called. The troopers had swapped their uniforms for civilian clothes and as Alice noted, if nothing else, they all smelt alike, since bathing was a luxury to be enjoyed once in a few days in the Ruins.

'Where do you want the first squad to go?'

Arjun, Satish, a woman called Sheila who led one of the groups of Rats and Alice were huddled around a hand-drawn map showing the Ruins, the Deadland and a Forward Base just ten kilometers from the city center where a large detachment of Red Guards had set up. It took a second for Alice to realize that the question had been directed to her. She struggled to answer and then Arjun gently nudged her along.

'Maybe we could do it as you said last night. Okay?'

When the others had dispersed, Alice called Arjun aside.

'Arjun, I don't know much about leading so many people. I don't know what to do.'

Arjun smiled.

'Alice, whether you like it or not, everyone here expects you to lead them. They've all heard the stories and read the posts. Most of those are probably exaggerated, but there you have it.'

Alice started to protest.

'Look, all I want is to fight back for what happened to my own. That's all. If others want to join me, then we can work together, but I'm not so sure I like leading so many people and being responsible for them.'

Arjun looked at her, and perhaps realizing that he was talking to someone who would be not much older than the daughter he had lost in The Rising, softened his voice.

'Alice, you are more than just a leader for them. These people, me, all of us- have spent the last few years without any hope, just scratching for survival from one day to the next. You've given them something they had lost. Hope.'

Alice started to say something, but Arjun interrupted her.

'You're the one who lived among the Biters and uncovered their truth. You're the one who fought Red Guards all alone to save your people. You're the one who convinced a Zeus officer to change sides. You're the one who led hundreds of troopers to desert. And yes, you're the cause of the Deadland being firebombed. So you are already responsible for a lot, whether you like it or not.'

Alice sat down as it all sank in. How many thousands had died because of her one silly decision to jump into the hole after the Biter that had triggered all of this? She wished she could just undo everything. Life had never been easy, but it had been a damn sight better than what she had to deal with now, and as she looked at the dozens of men and women gathered around their camp, she wondered whether she was just going to lead all of them to their deaths as well?

She closed her eyes and her father's face flashed before her and she remembered his last words to her. He had somehow believed she could bear this burden of leading others. He had believed that she was more than just another young girl whose fate was in other's hands. If nothing else, she had to prove him right, to make his sacrifice mean something. He had given his life so that she could live, and had believed that by living, she could make a difference and make things better. She turned to Arjun, a new determination in her eyes.

'Without heavy weapons we have no hope of getting through their base defenses, so we need to get them out of their base.'

`Why would they come out of their base?'

'They want me. I will offer myself up as bait.'

Three days later, two vans sped out of the Ruins towards the Red Guards Forward Base which housed several dozen Red Guards who had been placed there as a forward patrol and were supplied daily by helicopter. What made it less than an easy target were the two remotely controlled Gatling guns mounted on its walls. Alice was in the second van, and just thirty minutes earlier, Satish had sent a message on his tablet saying that he and his men wanted to rejoin Zeus. They had managed to capture Alice and wanted a trade- Alice for their guaranteed safety. It was a gamble- there was always a chance that Appleseed and his masters would just kill Alice when they had the chance, but Alice knew that even more than her life, they craved the secrets she knew about the Biter's hidden bases and also the Queen and her vaccine. They were sure that the Red Guards already had drones overhead, so they did not risk going too much into the open but stopped on the outskirts of the Ruins, roughly in the area where once a sprawling high-end complex had stood, housing guests and athletes for the Commonwealth Games held in Delhi some years before The Rising. The dried up Yamuna river was nearby and on Alice's instructions and unseen by any drones, more than three dozen fighters had crept through underground passages once used by the Queen's Biters.

They had timed it so that the Red Guards would not have time to bring in too many reinforcements but they could never be sure, so Alice felt her hands shake a bit as she got out of the van. She felt totally exposed as Satish and his men walked her into the open. They had all put on their Zeus uniforms and were fully armed while she had her hands loosely bound behind her. She could just about make out the Red Guards base, which had been set up inside what had once been a large temple. She could see the two round turrets on top of the walls and she struggled to control her panic as she saw a black helicopter rise from within the complex and fly towards them. The helicopter came to a hover some distance away and she could see the large red star painted on its side. The door slid open and she saw several Red Guards inside with their rifles pointed downwards. A voice called out over a loudspeaker.

'Send the girl forward alone and lay down your weapons. Other Red Guards are on their way to take you to our base. You have nothing to fear.'

Alice was pushed forward and she walked, her face downcast, towards the waiting helicopter, wondering if the bullet that would kill her was on the way.

TWELVE

ALICE SAW THE HELICOPTER COME lower till it was only a few dozen feet above the ground. The rotor wash was so strong it felt like it would blow her away and she had to keep her eyes half closed since she could not bring her hands up to shield them against the swirling wind and dust. She heard a dull roar in the distance and looked to her right to see two armored personnel carriers emerge from the Red Guards base and speed towards her location. The helicopter came even lower and landed on the road only a few meters away from Alice. She watched three Red Guards disembark, their rifles pointed at the Zeus troopers behind her. As she turned, she saw that Satish and the others had put their hands behind their heads and their rifles were on the ground in front of them. Apparently satisfied that they posed no immediate threat, a Red Guard officer emerged from the helicopter and pointed towards Alice.

'Come here!'

Alice walked slowly towards the helicopter, wondering if she would survive long enough to get a shot at the revenge she so badly wanted. As she saw the smirk on the Chinese officer's face, she had to struggle to contain the fury she felt inside. So many thousands of innocent men, women and children had been killed so that men like this could retain the power they so craved. The officer turned to Satish and shouted.

'We'll take her with us. My men are on the way in the APCs to take you in.'

Alice was sure that if the APCs did get close enough, their orders were to slaughter the Zeus deserters, but her whole plan hinged on them never getting close enough in the first place. They had not really planned on there being a helicopter at the scene, but now as Alice walked closer, she smiled. It was unplanned, but it could be a bonus. They had planned on bloodying the nose of the Red Guards enough to provoke them to try and enter the Ruins. But if they managed to take a helicopter and an officer, it would certainly add more insult to the injury. Of course, to do any of that, Alice had to improvise a bit and hope that she stayed alive long enough to cause any damage.

She was now just five feet or so away from the helicopter and she stopped, as if weighing her decision. The Red Guard officer was now cajoling her to come closer, an absurd gesture since Alice wondered why he'd think anyone would willingly step towards torture and near certain death. When she did not budge, he began to lose his patience and asked one of his men to go get her. The Red Guard started walking towards her and Alice looked right, hoping that Arjun and his Rats would not let her down. She watched the two APCs now barely five hundred meters away and closing in fast when the first APC was obscured by a giant cloud of smoke. A split second later, she heard the blast of the IED. She knew Arjun had triggered it prematurely since he wanted to create a distraction and give her a chance at getting away. He and his Rats were in tunnels around the road and even before the smoke from the explosion had cleared, she heard the sound of rifles firing as they attacked the APCs.

The Red Guard was now just a couple of feet from her and he had stopped to look at the explosion. He jerked his head around to look at Alice, but he was too late. Alice had slipped her hands out of the loose ropes binding them behind her, and now had a knife in her right hand and a pistol in her left. She jumped high and brought her knife down on the Red Guard's neck. As he went down, she didn't try and dislodge her knife, but left it there, rolling on the ground and coming up in a crouch, the handgun in both hands. She fired four or five rounds at the two Red Guards outside the helicopter and saw at least one fall, before she saw the officer bring up his own sidearm. She rolled under the helicopter as one of the Red Guards fired, the bullets kicking up the dust around her. She felt something hit her shoulder but kept going as the officer screamed.

'Stop, you idiot! You'll hit the helicopter.'

She came up on the other side of the helicopter and saw the officer turn to face her. He was way too late. She fired through the open helicopter cabin and put two rounds in his chest and clambered into the helicopter as she saw Satish and his men firing and the Red Guard outside fall to the ground. She peered into the cockpit and saw the pilot reaching for a pistol at his side.

'Not a good idea.'

He put his hands up, and she dragged him outside where his hands were tied by Satish's men. Alice saw that a fierce firefight was still raging on the road. The first APC was in flames, but the second one seemed undamaged and was backing away towards the base as rifle rounds pinged off it.

'Let's get out of here as soon as we can!'

Alice knew that when news spread that a helicopter

had been lost, the Red Guards would be back in force. She looked at Satish.

'Any of you guys know how to fly this thing?'

Satish shook his head and smiled. It was a tempting thought, but even if none of them could fly the helicopter, it still was a treasure trove for them. Within fifteen minutes, they crawled back through the tunnels, bringing with them the Red Guard pilot, weapons and communication equipment taken from the fallen Red Guards and most exciting for all of them, two RPG launchers they found in the helicopter, together with eight rockets.

Not only had they dealt a serious blow to the Red Guards' pride, but they had in one stroke, suddenly exponentially increased the firepower of their arsenal.

That night was one of open celebration, and one of slightly more hidden anxiety. Many of the men and women were drinking and singing, and Alice wondered where all the alcohol had materialized from. Arjun was sitting next to her, looking quite grim.

'Don't ask. People still scavenge and find stuff and some of the more adventurous ones make their own hooch. I wouldn't drink it if I wanted to be sure I'd still be walking the next day. Alice, they have tasted their first real victory so they are celebrating, but we need to think ahead.'

Alice had considered how the Red Guards would retaliate and she was well aware of the devastation they had wreaked in the Deadland so she looked at Arjun.

'Will they just bomb the Ruins like they did the Deadland?'

Satish had come up to join them and he replied.

'No, it's not as easy to bomb targets in an urban environment like this. Delhi was a huge city and even if most buildings are no longer standing, there are just too many places to hide for them to be sure they'll hit anything or anyone with an air strike.'

Arjun was still looking worried so Satish asked him what was on his mind.

'You and Alice are both too young to remember what happened after The Rising. I saw the Great Fires and what nuclear weapons did to our world. Why wouldn't the Red Guards just drop a nuke on the Ruins and finish us all?'

A chill went up Alice's spine. She had only heard stories of what those terrible weapons had done to whole cities in the madness that had followed The Rising. Having seen what supposedly `ordinary' bombs had done to the Deadland, she wondered what horrors nuclear weapons could unleash if they were indeed used. She noticed that Satish had a broad smile, something she could not fathom given the grim conversation they were having.

'Satish, what's got you in such a good mood?'

'Alice, our Chinese friend there is talking, and he has a lot to say about the way the world is now and what's on the Central Committee's mind. There's one big reason they won't risk nuking us, and it's the same big reason they're still trying to get human settlements under their control.'

When Alice looked at him with a raised eyebrow, he simply replied.

'Food.'

~ * * * ~

The Red Guard pilot was in a darkened basement and when Arjun stepped in with the torch in his hand, the pilot shielded his eyes. Alice and Satish followed and sat down around the pilot. He was still in uniform and Alice could see that he was bleeding from a cut on his lip. She spun towards Arjun.

'Who hit him?'

He put his hands up defensively.

'One of the guys got overenthusiastic and I

reminded them gently how you wanted prisoners treated.'

Alice grinned. Arjun's gentle persuasion would likely have included a solid blow to the gut. Satish was talking to the pilot in a foreign language and turned to Alice to explain.

'We all had to learn a bit of Mandarin to be able to communicate with Red Guard officers, but he can speak passable English.'

The pilot now took a closer look at Alice and flinched.

'The Yellow Haired Witch.'

Alice was shocked. She was aware that the Red Guards knew of her and were hunting her, but she had never imagined that they would have such a name for her.

'The name is Alice, Colonel Li. Now tell me what you know.'

An hour later, Arjun, Satish and Alice were sitting outside. For some minutes, none of them spoke as they were all digesting what they had learnt. It turned out that the pilot they had captured was much more valuable than they had imagined. Commander Jiang Li was not only a highly decorated Red Guard pilot, but was the son of Comrade Jemin Li, one of the most senior members of the Central Committee in Shanghai. As a Red Guard pilot of his rank, he would probably not have had much information beyond immediate tactical information on bases and weapons, which Alice would have taken to be very valuable in and of themselves. But being the son of such an important person meant that Commander Li was a treasure trove of information about what was happening in the outside world.

It turned out that most of the world had been utterly devastated by The Rising and the chaos that followed. What had been China's larger cities remained largely intact as many of those in bigger cities had been put in hardened shelters, but the countryside and smaller towns had been ravaged both by The Rising and retaliatory American strikes. It had been a desperate plan, one which Commander Li's father had been privy to, but with deep worldwide recession, China's economy tottering behind the US defaulting on debt, two years of famines, and growing calls for reform and democracy in China, some of those in power had taken a last gamble. What the planners behind the whole operation had never bargained for was the way the virus mutated and the way the Biters spread out of control. That together with the smaller tit for tat nuclear exchanges in Asia and the Middle East meant that while the Central Committee in China was the one relatively organized political force to remain standing, it ruled over a planet that was little more than a pile of ashes.

And also it now had more than two hundred million mouths to feed in China. In the first few years, they had been content to follow the Central Committee unquestioningly driven by their terror at what lay beyond the iron grip of the Committee and its Red Guards. However, over time, as food shortages set in, the Central Committee had to seek out remaining fertile lands and people to work those fields. Only two major food baskets of the world remained- what had been the the heartlands of the US and India. The Americans never gave up, and ever since the first Red Guards landed, had been waging a terrible guerilla war that was bleeding the Red Guards dry. Then they turned to the Deadland of North India, subcontracting Zeus to bring human settlements under their control as a source of labor for farms in India and China.

Alice had grown up seeing little beyond the immediate concerns of her family and settlement and being worried about little more than her immediate survival. It was a bit hard at first for her to grasp the true scale of the struggle they were a part of. But a life spent surviving meant that her instincts were razor sharp and she looked at both Satish and Arjun.

'First, if this Li is the son of such an important man, they will not hit us from the air. They will try and negotiate or come on the ground. We need to be ready.'

Arjun nodded, a slight smile on his face as he realized that the young girl everyone saw as their leader was taking charge.

'Second, if food and people to work the farms is what is so critical to them, we need to hit them where it hurts. No food will mean their own people will start turning against the Central Committee.'

She saw Satish hesitate, so she continued.

'Yes, I know it's harsh and some people may starve, but we cannot be soft. Finally, we need to find some way of coordinating with the Americans if we can.'

She had not told any of the others about the vial of the vaccine she carried, but while much of India had been reduced to the Deadland, she hoped that the Americans might still have people and facilities available where they could put the vaccine to some use. She had no idea of how they could contact the Americans or how they could be of any use to each other from half way across the world, but the knowledge that other people were waging the same war against the same enemy gave her hope and made her own effort feel less lonely.

Just two days later, the first strike in Alice's plan was put into motion.

'Queen of Hearts, I am at the dinner table.'

Alice clicked her mike once by way of acknowledgement and then looking at the airfield spread out in front of her.

'King of Hearts, is the Knave in position?'

She heard a click from Arjun affirming that Satish and his men were also ready. Once Arjun had heard of the book that the Queen carried with her and the prophecy associated with it, he had suggested the code names. That had brought about much laughter among the older folks there, though Alice, never having read the book, really didn't know where the names came from. They were about fifty kilometers from their base in the Ruins, near what had once been the international airport at Delhi. It was now a small, barely serviceable airfield, but it was the key lifeline through which local settlers were sent to farms in China and also produce grown in farms around the region were sent to storage depots the Central Committee controlled. Alice could see three large transport aircraft and two helicopters there through her binoculars. There were several guard towers, at least two of which had remotely controlled gun turrets, and she could see many armed Red Guards walking along the airfield perimeter.

It was clearly too heavily defended to attack in a frontal assault, but that was not Alice's intent. The heist from the Red Guards helicopter had proved to be quite valuable, and together with what the Zeus deserters had bought with them, they now not only had far superior firepower but also many more tactical radios to help in their communication. Alice was sure their transmissions were being intercepted which was why they were using the code names Arjun had thought up.

'The Knave sees some tarts on the table.'

That meant that Satish and his men had seen the convoy approaching them from their position about five kilometers away. They were dug in below the ruins of what had once been crisscrossing flyovers that had provided easy access to the airport from the city. With a combination of the rage among the remaining human settlements in the Deadland after the air raids and the increasing desertions among Zeus troopers, the intelligence they had on Red Guard movements had increased exponentially. So today, Alice knew that three APCs would be escorting a convoy of trucks packed with settlers to be flown to labor camps in China. Her intent was not to hurt the settlers but to take out the APCs and free the settlers. That was the job that fell to Satish and his crew. She, Arjun and a dozen others were to wreak some havoc at the airfield.

Satish's next transmission came ten minutes later. It was simple and terse.

'The Knave of Hearts, he stole some tarts.'

Alice smiled. That meant his part of the mission had been accomplished. Now she would have to put into motion her own plan. Word of the raid must have gotten to the airfield because she saw several Red Guards clamber onto APCs and two helicopter gunships begin to take off. Alice and the others had made their way to their positions two days ago, traveling largely underground, through old sewers, and often lying still in the filth for hours when Red Guard patrols flew overhead. It had been a hard journey, but now it was all going to pay off. As the helicopters approached their position, Alice spoke into her radio.

'King of Hearts, beat them sore.'

She saw two smoke trails emerge from the ground across the road from her as RPGs snaked out towards the approaching helicopters. One missed its mark, but the other hit the lead helicopter just behind the cockpit. The helicopter seemed to shudder in mid-flight and then began to spin out of control as it crashed to the ground. The second helicopter began to turn towards this sudden threat when Alice screamed at her men to fire. Two more rockets flew towards the helicopter and Alice shouted in triumph as they both struck home. There was a fireball and the helicopter seemed to break into two as it fell. As Alice saw four APCs speed out of the airport gates, she was tempted to wreak some more damage, but she knew that standing and fighting in the open would mean heavy casualties. So they retreated back to their underground tunnels and began the journey back to the Ruins.

~ * * * ~

When Alice got back, the first thing she did was to sleep, trying to make up for the three days she had just been through with barely any rest. When she awoke, Satish told her that they had managed to destroy the APCs accompanying the convoy and liberate more than three hundred settlers. The men and women, all angry at the casualties they knew the air raids had caused at other settlements and at being taken away from their families, were keen to join in the struggle against the Red Guards. When Alice walked out of her room she saw a sight she was not at all prepared for.

More than five hundred people were gathered among the ruins of buildings that had once been a posh apartment complex. It was almost Sunset so a few torches had been lit. She was about to ask Arjun whether it was smart for so many of them to be in the open when a huge roar welcomed her. A man walked up to her.

'My name is Swapnil and I led our settlement near Mehrauli. Thank you for rescuing us. Some of us would want to go back to our families but I and many others will fight for you in your army. Just tell us what you need.'

As Alice looked around her, she considered what the man had said. Did she indeed now have an army? To think that so many people depended on her, and looked to her for direction was a scary thought but at the same time, she felt an intense surge of pride. If only her father could have seen her now. He had lived and died so that his people could continue to live free, and now she was finally in a position to not just avenge his death but to try and fight for what he had believed in. The celebrations were short-lived because having so many people in the open was an invitation for an air strike. Alice was sure that the Red Guards would be furious at the loss of three helicopters in just a few days and a threat to what they had taken to be an assured source of supply for their labor camps would cause them to lash out. Add to that the fact that the son of a senior Central Committee official was a prisoner in the Ruins, and she was sure that they would take some action, and soon.

She did not have to wait long. She was in a second floor room in what had once been an apartment when she heard the dull roar of approaching helicopters. She had lookouts on the nearby rooftops and soon enough she saw RPGs reach out towards the helicopters. In the darkness it was hard to see how close they came but without any signs of explosions, they seemed to have missed. Explosions rocked one of the rooftops as missiles fired in retaliation found their mark, and Alice wondered which of her comrades she had just lost.

'King of Hearts, Knave of Hearts. Time to go down the Rabbit Hole.'

Their plan was simple. It would be suicide to engage helicopter gunships with just RPGs and small arms. So, with the initial volley of RPGs they had got the Red Guards interested, but now they would hunker down and wait for the Red Guards to make the next move. The whole plan was to get them on the ground where they could be fought on more even terms. Alice watched at least a half dozen helicopters hover near the ground as black figures slithered down ropes. Part of her pitied the Red Guards, who were probably ordinary soldiers being forced into an impossible mission because the son of an important man was at stake. But she reasoned that they were doing their job, and she would do hers. Through the night vision scope on her rifle she watched the Red

Guards sweep from one building to another. Commander Li was in the same building as her, sitting in the basement parking lot with four men guarding him. He did not have much more by way of intelligence to offer up, but he was a valuable bargaining chip and their best bet that the Red Guards would not just level the entire neighborhood with air strikes.

She watched a four man team of the Red Guards approach the building in front of her, across a small park where perhaps years ago, children would have played. Even today, a slide remained as a memorial to those simpler, happier days. Under that slide was what appeared to be a garbage bin. Inside it was an IED that Alice had rigged. As the Red Guards passed by the slide, she connected the two wires in front of her. The IED went off with a huge explosion that was deafening in the quiet of the night. When she put her scope back to her eyes, she saw all four Red Guards down. The others were now scrambling for cover, and one or two had fired, likely panicking and firing at shadows. Their muzzle flashes gave them away and they were met with a withering volley of rifle and RPG fire from men and women hidden in the Ruins around them. Alice saw a Red Guard run across the park, perhaps separated from his squad in the chaos. She took careful aim and fired a single round, bringing him down with a shot to the leg. As he scrambled on all fours, two shadows emerged from the darkness and took him away. The helicopters were buzzing overhead like angry hornets, but with the Red Guards mixed up in close combat, there was little they could do. One of them tried to come lower, but a near miss from an RPG sent it back up.

The firing went on for about twenty minutes and then there was silence. As per her plan, nobody cheered, and nobody went out to celebrate. In stark contrast to the deafening crescendo of gunfire and explosions that had rocked the complex just minutes ago, there was now no sound to be heard other than the helicopters overhead. Alice wondered if they would have called for reinforcements, but when and if they arrived they would find an abandoned apartment complex with nothing there but the bodies of a dozen or so Red Guards and multiple booby traps to make life interesting for any Red Guard who landed.

Alice and everyone with her, including eight Red Guards who had been captured alive, were already on their way through the Ruins and its underground tunnels to another hideout.

The deadly game of cat and mouse that was to be played in the Ruins had begun in earnest.

THIRTEEN

TWO MORE WEEKS PASSED, WHERE not a single day went by without a raid by Red Guards. After their initial heavy losses in the house to house fighting in the Ruins, the Red Guards were increasingly using drones and air strikes. While that meant fewer Red Guard losses, it also meant that casualties on the side of Alice and her teams were also lower, because it was easy to hide in the Ruins or in the warren of underground tunnels and sewers. Alice realized early that they did not have the numbers or firepower to engage the Red Guards in open combat, so they would hide in the Ruins and use IEDs and ambushes to extract as heavy a toll as possible. Alice's army had also been bolstered by increasing defections among Zeus troopers, and while in absolute the numbers may have been low, the experience some of the recent defectors brought with them helped increase their capabilities and knowledge exponentially. Some of them were senior officers who had been Lieutenants or Majors in the Indian Army before The Rising, and they began a series of classroom trainings. Alice was fascinated by what she learnt. Her knowledge of combat had been forged in the Deadland, where the best schooling was learning to survive every day. But now she learnt of past battles in the Old World, of how insurgents in countries held off mighty armies with air power using low-tech IEDs and ambushes. She learnt of counter-insurgency and quickly grasped how much the Red Guards had bungled in alienating the local people. That was something she immediately set about capitalizing on.

Often in the darkness of night, she and a small group would travel into the Deadland and meet with settlements, telling them of the struggle that was being waged and asking them for their support. Alice had thought that telling them about how evil the Red Guards were and the conspiracy behind The Rising would be enough to get the settlements on her side, but it wasn't always so easy. One evening, Arjun sat down next to her.

'Alice, only a few people will fight out of a desire for revenge. Maybe some people like you who have directly lost family and friends to the Red Guards. But others want safety for their families, and they won't be motivated only by wanting to destroy something, but the promise of something that is a better life.'

Alice had never thought of it that way.

'Arjun, how do you know so much about this?'

He smiled.

'Remember, I was a salesman. My job was selling things to people which they often didn't want, and the key is that we need to make them want something they may not even have considered before.'

'What would they want?'

Arjun took out a faded photograph. It showed a city street with cars and people walking around.

'Most of the leaders of the settlements were young men and women before The Rising. They remember how life was before, and if you ask all of them, including me, what they would most want- they would say that they want the safety and stability that they once had. Especially in places like India and the US which were democracies, people would want to be able to choose their future instead of having someone sitting in Shanghai deciding it for them.'

Democracy.

Alice had never seen what the Old World had been like, but her father had often talked about the ideals he had believed in, and things he had tried so hard to bring to life in their own settlement. A system where people did not rule because they were stronger or better armed, but where people chose those who would guide them, and decisions were taken by voting on them. She knew that the heavy-handed tactics of Zeus had rankled among a lot of the settlements but they had been happy to trade freedom for safety. Could she really offer them an alternative? The tactics of the Red Guards and defections among Zeus troopers had certainly made them question what they were actually signing up for when they accepted the supposed safety of operating under the Red Guards umbrella, especially when Commander Li had revealed the inhuman conditions in the labor camps were people from the settlements were taken. But what kind of life could she offer in the desolation of the Deadland or the Ruins?

Arjun must have read her mind.

'Alice, there are now more than five hundred of us. All of us living in the Ruins. Families, people who till a day ago were strangers, all living together. Think about what we've started here.'

The next day saw several Red Guard sorties over the Ruins. Jets and helicopters seemed to be dropping bombs and firing rockets, but they were nowhere near Alice and her troops. Alice thought they must have been acting on faulty intelligence and the misguided air raid of the Red Guards was the subject of many a joke over lunch.

Alice was leading a patrol in the Ruins the next

night with two of Satish's men when a threat that she had almost forgotten about presented itself. One of the young Zeus troopers ahead suddenly screamed and Alice was instantly on guard, bringing up her night vision scope to her eyes. She saw three shapes emerge from behind the building in front of her. From the way they moved, there was no doubt that they were Biters. The trooper was lying at their feet, his neck bent at an impossible angle. She heard a sound to her left and turned to see three more Biters emerge. Alice hesitated for only a minute, as she thought of the Queen and the Biters who had helped her before squeezing the trigger on her rifle, sending the first Biter down with a bullet to the head. The others charged at her and she shot another before she ordered the trooper with her to retreat. In such close quarters, and not knowing how many other Biters were around, standing and fighting would be suicidal. She ran through the darkness, more than once swerving away from what she thought was a Biter lurking in the shadows but turned out to be a pipe or a broken piece of furniture.

'Vivek, you with me?'

She got no reply from the trooper and just hoped that he was okay. A Biter suddenly appeared in front of her, and without breaking her stride she hit him on the face with the butt of her rifle and as he went down, fired a round into his head. Knowing that she was probably too far from her base to be able to make it in the darkness while she was surrounded by Biters, she made for the nearest intact building and clambered up the stairs to the second floor. She huddled against the wall, her rifle trained at the stairs. She had two fragmentation grenades with her, so if the Biters did try and attack in force, she would give them a nice surprise. She saw a Biter appear in the doorway and a single round to the head put him down. Two more followed and she fired again, missing twice but then compensating with two more head shots that put them down. She retreated further up the stairs and hoped she had not drawn too much attention to herself.

When no more Biters presented themselves for a few seconds, she breathed a bit easy and looked out the window through her scope. She saw the flag that Arjun had put up, partially hidden behind an old lamppost. She thanked the Red Guards for their high technology scopes since it told her precisely that their base was two thousand meters away. She didn't know if she wanted to risk trying to walk alone in the darkness with an unknown number of Biters around so she took out her tactical radio to call Arjun for assistance. That was when several gunshots shattered the silence of the night. There were a few scattered single shots but then someone began firing on full automatic. The gunshots were coming from the direction of their base, and as Alice looked through her scope, she could see several muzzle flashes. Sweeping her scope around, she saw several dark shadows shuffling towards the base and she knew what the Red Guards had done. They did not have to land and fight house to house after all. They had stirred up the Biters by bombing them, and now the Biters were streaming towards the areas where the humans were based. Alice gripped her rifle and prepared to rush to her friends' aid.

The Red Guards had just opened a new, deadly front in the war in the Ruins.

~ * * * ~

When Alice reached her base, she saw several Biters lying on the ground, their heads shattered by direct hits. However, when she got closer she noted with dismay that many of her team were also dead. The Biters had taken them totally by surprise. Used to days of airborne attacks by the Red Guards, they had never really anticipated a ground attack by Biters. She saw Arjun point his pistol at a writhing man on the ground and shoot him in the head. Better dead than undead was a fine slogan, but from the pain in Arjun's face, she knew how tough it was to have to shoot a friend.

She saw Satish running, his rifle in hand, screaming to his men.

'Get snipers on the roofs now. Watch for any stragglers!'

He stopped in front of Alice.

'They caught us with our pants down, Alice.'

Alice looked at the devastation around her and asked how bad their losses were.

'As best as I can tell, we lost eight or nine people.'

'Also we cannot stay here any longer. If the Biters are being driven from their hiding places and coming into our areas, we need to find a place that can be more easily fortified and defended.'

'But that makes us a more visible target for air strikes, right?'

Arjun gave a wan smile, showing that he knew well the kind of dilemma the Red Guards had placed them in. The next morning was a dark one, where they buried their dead, which in itself was a tough decision for many of the Hindus among them. Funeral pyres would have been a beacon for air strikes to home in on. Then they began the search for a new stronghold.

After more than an hour of walking through the Ruins, Alice clicked twice on her radio. To avoid attracting attention, they had spread out into five separate smaller groups, and now gradually they would converge where Alice was.

'This is such a visible target, Alice. Are you sure we should be here?'

Alice smiled at Arjun.

'Take a look around. There are so many underground parking lots and rooms that nobody could really take us out from the air. With our friend

Li and the other prisoners, I doubt they'd use any heavier weapons. Also its walls mean that we can set up defenses against any Biters or Red Guards coming from outside.'

They were inside what had once been a large sports stadium. The bleachers around the stadium were all long devastated but the huge sloping roof was still largely intact and hid the giant field and rooms below.

One of the former Zeus officers walked up and whistled.

'Good idea, Alice. This is a perfect headquarters for us, but as more and more people join us, I'd like to see them set up homes in the adjoining buildings. These were once built to house thousands of athletes during some big events. Take a look- many of them are still livable, and being close to the stadium means that we can still create a safety net for each other, but they also get some space for themselves and their families.'

'Makes a lot of sense.'

Within a week, the stadium started becoming the focal point for what was essentially the beginning of the resettlement of the Ruins that had once been Delhi. Word spread and people began walking in, at first in small groups, and then entire settlements from the Deadland. Alice was suddenly seized with all the administrative challenges that came with taking care of more than a thousand people who essentially depended on her. Luckily, there were enough people around with skills from the Old World who could help. A former Accountant took charge of maintaining inventories of food and supplies. Satish took charge of base security, which consisted of ensuring security for the stadium and for all the families now settling around it. Several of the settlers jury-rigged generators powered with fuel that could still be easily scavenged in the Ruins and now the main eating and meeting rooms in the stadium had electricity, and there was already talk of extending that to all the apartments occupied by families.

Arjun and his Rats took charge of what he called forward security, which meant venturing deeper into the Ruins to look for supplies and also find other humans. Within days, their community numbered in the thousands, and Alice's legend seemed to only grow in the telling. One day, Alice confided to Arjun that she felt bad that a lot of the things people believed about her were not true. For example, she most certainly had not destroyed an APC single-handedly. Arjun smiled and told her that her legend was one of the glues that was binding everyone together, and if it could help achieve such a wonderful thing, it was perhaps best left alone.

In the daily meetings that Alice called where people could talk about issues and ideas to make their lives better, an old lady asked her a question that perplexed her.

'Alice, what should we call this little town of ours?'

It was then that Alice remembered the charred book that the Queen had carried with her and how much it had meant to her. She had heard nothing of the Queen since she had slipped away, and thought it may be a fitting way to remember her, so she said that their community be called Wonderland.

There was raucous laughter, especially among many of the old folks who knew the fairy tale. It was hardly an uneventful period. Red Guard sorties continued daily, and every once in a while, a helicopter pilot would fire a rocket or two but given the thick stadium roof and their dug in positions, these caused little damage. Air raids also started to lessen when the Red Guard pilots realized that some defecting Zeus troopers had taken with them man portable anti-aircraft missiles looted from armories. These had been positioned in the tallest buildings around the area and while Alice knew that they did not have enough if the Red Guards mounted a large scale attack, she also knew that the cost of any such attack would be prohibitive. So an uneasy peace came to exist between them and the Red Guards, and at least for the short term, Wonderland knew some measure of security from attacks by the Red Guards.

The Red Guards however continued their raids on the areas where Biters were said to be, and much like hunters driving wild animals, they continued driving Biters towards the stadium. The difference was that now in a clearly fortified position with lots of adjoining buildings that provided a perfect location for snipers and overlapping fields of fire, the occasional hordes of Biters that appeared were dealt with at long range, well before they could cause any damage. While Alice felt a bit bad about taking out what she knew were not really evil monsters but perhaps something closer to rabid animals, the safety of those who depended on her was the most important thing on her mind.

When she felt that they were settled in their new base, she began to set two plans in motion.

The first was a renewed campaign against the supply lines of the Red Guards. Arjun volunteered to lead that effort, and there was no shortage of volunteers from the settlements in the Deadland who were eager to take revenge against the Red Guards. The second was a more challenging endeavor- that of establishing communication with the outside world. One of the deserting Zeus officers had brought along a shortwave radio and they set up a communications centre in what had been once been the broadcast room in the stadium. Alice sat there and listened to what seemed to be an endless hiss of static before she gave up. They had much more success with what one of the former Zeus officers called Information Warfare. They used the many tablets they had brought with them and the tablets captured from the Red Guards to bombard the Red Guard and Zeus Intranets with messages of their ongoing struggle. Within a week, the

Zeus Intranet was down, a sure sign that the Red Guards had lost almost all command and control over what had once been their primary instrument for maintaining control in the Deadland of India. Zeus deserters spoke of open mutiny and warfare and of whole units of deserting Zeus troopers being slaughtered in air strikes by the Red Guards. However that also meant that more and more Red Guards were streaming into the Deadlands and they were bringing with them heavier weaponry.

Then one day, Alice walked into the communications room and was told that they had a very unexpected and surprising message.

It was a message from the Central Committee.

~ * * * ~

That night, as they all gathered in the underground parking lot of the stadium, the tension and excitement in the air was palpable. There were a couple of lamps powered by their generator that threw off ghostly shadows on the wall lending the proceedings an even more eerie air.

'Alice, it could all be a trick.'

Arjun had said the words quietly, and Alice was thankful that he was not openly challenging her, but she also knew that he was saying what was on the minds of many of those gathered before her. Alice turned to the crowd assembled in front of her.

'Everyone, we received a message from the Central Committee earlier today.'

Everyone had been speculating all day what the special announcement was, and now that it was out in the open, all conversation died down, all eyes trained on Alice as she continued.

'They are proposing a cease fire.'

Several people in the audience applauded, and that told Alice a lot. After years of fighting for survival, they had begun to find a sense of safety and community in Wonderland. A cease fire would mean that they could at least continue the process of rebuilding their lives and expanding their community without fear of attack. Alice held up her hand and everyone was quiet again.

'Their terms are that we release Commander Li and all the dozen other Red Guards we hold prisoner and that we cease all attacks on their supply lines. In return, they commit to not launch any attacks on our base here in Wonderland.'

She heard several in the crowd mutter about how the Central Committee could not be trusted and she realized that just as with her and Arjun, opinion was divided.

Alice spoke more loudly and the voices in the crowd died down.

'I know as well as all of you of what we have lost to the Red Guards and their masters. So I have no desire to surrender to them or leave ourselves vulnerable. But there is something more than fighting to survive, there has to be. I was born in the Deadland and knew a life where all I had to look forward to was living one more day, but many of you remember a life before The Rising, a life where there was more to look forward to.'

She knew she had struck a chord and felt all eyes in the crowd on her as she continued.

'Many of you follow me, and I'm not sure I deserve all that trust, but I do know I've seen and felt something different in the last few weeks. We are now no longer just a band of fighters in hiding. We are more than that- we are starting to create a community. A community where we have laws, security, where children don't have to grow up afraid of the dark as I was. A friend once told me that we needed something more than just a common enemy to stick together, and I think we're beginning to find it- a place called home, a place we can run the way we want. A place we all call Wonderland.'

Several in the crowd shouted in approval and when she looked at Arjun, he was smiling.

'I don't like or trust the Red Guards any more than you, but it's clear that we don't have the firepower or numbers to really take the battle to them, and they know they can't wipe us out without drastic measures like nuclear weapons, and that would risk the very fertile lands they rely on to feed their people. So I will agree to stop attacks on their supply routes in return for a temporary cease fire, and I will let our prisoners return.'

Several in the crowd began to mutter angrily when Alice raised a hand to silence them.

'Only those prisoners will return who want to. Others will remain with us as our guests and over time, a part of our community.'

She motioned to her left and Commander Li walked onto the raised platform, eliciting many gasps of surprise. He spoke in halting English, but what he said electrified everyone.

'I was a pilot in the Red Guards, and I believed we were fighting to protect our people from the monsters you call Biters and to help secure areas to feed our people. I've spent enough time here and seen enough documents that make me question that. So I and three of my comrades have chosen to stay here. I know this war cannot be fought to victory by either side, but with the influence my father has and through my words, I hope I can help bring some sort of a workable peace.'

Arjun was looking at Alice in surprise. While he had been out raiding, she had been at work, talking to Li and trying to convince him of all that she herself had discovered not too long ago. Alice knew there was a risk that the Central Committee would denounce Li as a traitor and they would lose the leverage they had, but she was counting on the fact that they would choose to believe that he was being kept prisoner as a pawn for further negotiations.

Alice concluded by saying that they vote on it. This was her first real experience of what people called democracy, and she was nervous that the idea would split the group. Instead, she saw a near unanimous acceptance of the proposal.

Alice walked away with slightly conflicted feelings. On the one hand, part of her felt that her vengeance for the deaths of her family and friends was incomplete, and wanted to continue the battle. On the other hand, she now felt responsible for the thousands of people who depended on her, and didn't want to throw away their lives for her personal vengeance. Arjun walked up to her.

'Alice, you did a very brave thing. When I first met you, you were an angry young girl looking for revenge. Today, you are a young woman whom I'd be led by any day.'

The next day was spent preparing for the swap. Eight Red Guard prisoners were to be escorted by Alice, Arjun and close to fifty heavily armed men. Four of them were carrying man-portable SAMs and would be traveling in jeeps and taking up position slightly behind the group in case of any surprise air attacks. The meeting point was deeper in the Deadland, close to where the malls and offices had been in the suburb called Noida. As they passed the area, Alice saw the shattered remains of a giant statue that she had been told had once been a statue of the Hindu God Shiva. It was fitting that it lay in ruins along with the Old World it represented.

'Alice, you should not have come.'

It was not the first time Arjun had suggested it, but she was not going to send so many of her people into harm's way without being there to share the risks with them. And if this decision was going to mean that the people of Wonderland could enjoy at least a few days of peace, then it was worth it. As they reached the rendezvous point, near the ruins of what had once supposedly been one of the largest shopping malls in the city, Alice gawked at it for a few seconds, imagining what it must have been like to walk into a building and buy whatever you wanted- food, clothes, games- and walk out, without worrying about Biters or Red Guards.

She heard the helicopter before she saw it, and looked up to see a large transport helicopter approaching. As it came closer, she heard some of the men cocking their guns, and she whispered for them to not make any threatening moves. While she was trying to appear calm and composed, she was constantly fidgeting with the necklace she was wearing. Not knowing what else to do with the vial the Queen had given her, and also wanting to keep it safe, she had looped a chain through it and had been wearing it ever since the Queen disappeared. She saw the helicopter land a few meters away and a single officer got out and began walking towards her. She had to admire his courage for walking towards more than fifty heavily armed enemies all alone and seemingly unarmed. There were two snipers inside the helicopter but they made no move to get out of the helicopter or even to sight their weapons.

The officer now was close enough for her to hear and he stopped, speaking in impeccable English, and smiling slightly.

'So, you must be this Alice who has caused us so much trouble. I am General Chen of the Red Guards, and I have come to take possession of my men. Please have them walk towards me and then we will leave and fully honor the agreement we have made.'

Alice motioned to Arjun who nudged the Red Guard prisoners forward, and they began walking towards Chen. It was then that she noticed something odd. Chen had taken out a thin mask and was putting it on his face. She saw the two Red Guards in the helicopter lean out and fire something in the air. As she watched the small projectiles loop up in the air and fall towards them, she screamed to Arjun and the others to take cover.

She had her rifle up and was firing at the helicopter when the first projectile struck somewhere behind her. She saw one of the Red Guards twitch and fall as her bullets hit home and then she instinctively dove for cover as she heard an explosion behind her. When she looked back, she saw that it was not a grenade as she had feared. Instead, there was a greenish haze that was enveloping Arjun and the others, who were grabbing their necks and falling to the ground. Arjun tried to raise his rifle, but he seemed to gag and then fall to his knees. The wind was carrying the gas further away, and then she saw the men with the SAMs fall in their jeeps. She felt a burning sensation in her throat and started coughing violently, as if she were choking on something. Then she felt a boot on the small of her back. It was Chen.

'This one I want alive.'

Two masked Red Guards pulled her up and one of them put a mask on her face. If she had any notions of fighting back, they dissipated when one of them injected her with something that made her muscles go limp. She could see Chen standing there in front of her, and he pointed to the sky. When she looked up, she saw waves of heavy bombers headed south. Towards Wonderland. When she tried to struggle against the men holding her, one of them hit her in the head, knocking her out.

Her last thought was that yet again, she was going to fail those who had depended on her.

FOURTEEN

WHEN ALICE OPENED HER EYES, they were watering and her mouth was dry. She tried to bring her hands up but found that she could not move them. As she moved her head to look around, she found that she was lying on a bed and her hands and legs were tied down by thick belts. She was in a room where there was no other furniture other than a single metal chair and there were no windows, only a single door. When the door swung open, she saw a familiar shape walk in.

It was Appleseed.

Then the memory of what had happened kicked in, and she thrashed about on the bed, trying to free herself, trying to get at the men who had caused her so much loss. Appleseed calmly sat down on the chair next to her.

'Alice, it's no use. You should just relax.'

'What happened to Wonder...the people with me?'

Appleseed smiled.

'It's a miracle what two dozen heavy bombers, each carrying ten thousand pounds of fuel air explosives can do. I overflew the site of your so called Wonderland in a helicopter soon afterwards. Let's just say most, if not all your friends are burning in Hell, as they should.'

Alice felt hot tears streaming down her face.

'But, Commander Li and the others...'

Appleseed cut her off.

'Do you really think we would negotiate with you for one man, no matter whose son he might be? The Central Committee ordered the raid after Commander Li's father himself denounced him as a counter-revolutionary. The old man was forced to do it when the Central Committee figured they had a plan to kill or capture you. Now I hope you understand the kind of men I serve, and the kind of men you chose to pick a fight with.'

Alice cried silently at the loss of so many innocent lives and then spat at Appleseed, who flinched as the spittle hit his face.

'All we wanted to do was to be left alone. That's all any of us ever wanted.'

Appleseed wiped his face clean, but to Alice's surprise, there was no anger in his voice.

'Alice, don't you get it? It doesn't matter what you want or what your father wanted. If there's one thing you should learn from all this is that the world has always been ruled by a few powerful men. Men who brought about The Rising, men who make up the Central Committee, and don't for a moment think they're all Chinese. You'll be surprised who from the Old World is there- billionaire businessmen, bankers, Presidents, arms brokers- all part of one brotherhood that was planning for a day when the world would not have enough resources to support its population and when the masses would start turning against the power they held. We are just tools to get their work done. The sooner you reconcile to that, the longer your life will be.'

Alice wondered why he was confiding in her and what his masters wanted with her. Appleseed saw the question in her eyes.

'You are different. You became a visible symbol of opposition to them, and that started making other people think that there is a way to live in safety outside of the Central Committee's New World Order. It started giving people dangerous ideas about who and what the Biters may be, and whether they could actually be cured or assimilated. You were a public threat, and they will make a public spectacle of you. Tomorrow you are to be flown to Shanghai to be executed, and that execution will be broadcast live to all settlements in the New World.'

The prospect of death did not scare Alice as much as she had thought it might. Instead what scared her the most was the emptiness she felt inside. She literally had nothing or nobody to live for any more. She had failed those who had put their faith in her, believing naively that they could make a fresh start in a world where the only thing that mattered was power and everyone was but a puppet dancing to strings that were in the hands of the men who commanded Appleseed and Chen. She had never felt so bereft of hope before in her life, and cried for everything she had lost.

Appleseed walked over to her, resting his hand on her stomach. Something about his touch made her look at him.

'Get your hands off me!'

Appleseed smiled and leaned closer.

'I don't think you are in much of a position to tell me what to do. Do you realize just how much you have cost me? I lost my best men, and the army I once commanded is now hunted down by the Red Guards. I survived only because of my loyalty and because I personally helped track down and eliminate deserters.'

His hand was now moving up her body and Alice struggled against the belts holding her down in vain as his hand came to a stop just below her chest and he leaned down closer towards her face.

'Once, I would have been tempted with a young girl as attractive as you lying in front of me. I often wished that I could punish you for all you have done by making you beg and scream for mercy as I forced myself on you.'

Alice lay still, listening to Appleseed. She had already made up her mind. If he did try to rape her, he would have to undo at least one of the belts holding her legs together. Even with just one leg free, she would try and cause enough damage for him to be angry enough to end it all. She had heard the slogan better dead than undead many times in training, but she knew that sometimes, there were things worse than being undead, and being at the mercy of a brute like Appleseed was one of them. Appleseed paused.

'Now that you're in front of me, I just want to blow your brains out. Too bad I have to leave that pleasure to the folks in Shanghai. But at least I won't be deprived of all pleasure.'

Appleseed began loosening his belt when suddenly several shots rang out. Someone was firing on full automatic. The door burst open and a Red Guard walked in. When he saw Appleseed with his belt open, he paused till the General barked at him.

'Which idiot is firing outside?'

The Red Guard was ashen faced as he replied and Alice could see the fear in his eyes.

'Sir, we're under attack.'

Appleseed was irritated at having been interrupted and waved his hand to dismiss the Red Guard.

'An attack? We wiped most of those fools out in the Ruins two days ago. If it's a rabble of some insurgents, tell the men to get the choppers in the air and send out a squad of Guards. I'll be with you shortly.'

Appleseed had turned to face Alice again when she saw the Red Guard hesitate as he spoke again.

'Sir, we need you at the Command Centre. We've

never seen such an attack before.'

Appleseed turned on him in fury.

'What the hell is wrong with you? Don't you understand a simple order? Ok, tell me, who is attacking us?'

Alice saw the Red Guard's eyes widen and he spoke in what was barely a whisper.

'Sir, we're under attack by an army of Biters. Thousands and thousands of them.'

~ * * * ~

Alice watched the look of surprise on Appleseed's face as more shots rang out outside. She could see him hesitate for a moment before his face hardened.

'Thousands, my foot! Must be a band of Biters that has wandered our way. Come with me!'

As he went out of the room, Alice's relief at being spared was quickly replaced by anxiety about what was happening outside. She heard more gunshots and then she heard something that chilled her. It sounded like thousands of animals baying and roaring together, creating a bizarre symphony. She didn't know if there were actually thousands of Biters outside or not, but she had never heard so many of them together, and screaming with such ferocity that they could be heard above the din of gunfire. She then heard the buzz of helicopters taking off and then loud explosions as what she presumed were rockets streaked into the approaching Biters. She had grown up thinking of Biters as mindless monsters but had also seen them at close quarters as more like frightened, infected animals. She wondered what could be making them walk into a slaughter with the firepower that Appleseed and the Red Guards would have arrayed against them.

Then the room seemed to shake and Alice saw several bricks fall off the wall. Another loud explosion and the bed fell over on its side. Alice cried out as her head hit the floor and wondered why the Red Guards were firing on their own base. Another explosion seemed shook the base and she felt the belt holding one of her hands snap open as the bed shook from the impact. Alice quickly undid the other belts and then stepped towards the open door. The corridor outside did not seem to be guarded and so she walked down it and then peered around the corner where she saw what appeared to be a Command Centre with many display screens and a large window. It was from here that Appleseed and his staff seemed to be directing the battle. There were at least twenty staffers with Appleseed and they all seemed to be focusing out the window, so nobody saw her behind them.

When Alice looked out the window, she froze at the sight. There was a small courtyard with a helipad to one side, and then a high perimeter wall ringed by automatic gun turrets and guard towers. Outside the wall, as far as she could see, was a sea of approaching Biters. The Red Guard had been right- there must have been thousands of them, and while they were steadily being mowed down by fire from the turrets and rockets from two hovering helicopters, with their sheer weight of numbers, they kept closing in. Appleseed was screaming to his men.

'Morons! Biters don't fire RPGs. There are people mixed in among them.'

Alice saw several smoke trails from the mob of Biters outside and realized what had hit the building, freeing her in the process. Several RPGs reached out towards the perimeter wall and a guard tower was obliterated. A cheer went up from the mob outside, and Alice heard a few human voices mixed among the howls of the Biters. Part of her wondered how this army had been assembled and who was leading it, but for now she was transfixed by the battle unfolding before her. Appleseed was screaming at his men to pick off the humans in the army outside since they presented the biggest threat with the RPGs they were carrying but what was obvious to Alice was that this battle was already lost for Appleseed and his men. There were just too many Biters approaching to be taken out by two helicopters and the handful of Red Guards she saw, and clearly Appleseed's men had never anticipated that there would be humans with firearms mixed in among them. Appleseed was screaming as to why nobody had told him earlier when one of his subordinates blurted out.

'Sir, we saw only a dozen Biters and we thought our patrol outside could handle them. Then they started streaming out of holes in the ground.'

'Have you called in for air support?'

'Sir, they say close air fighters are airborne, but won't get here for at least another fifteen minutes.'

As Appleseed screamed out his rage, Alice looked outside and saw a jeep appear over the horizon, speeding towards the base. In the glow created by exploding rockets she saw a figure standing in the jeep, grey hair flowing behind her, holding aloft a book in one hand.

It was the Queen.

Appleseed had seen the jeep as well and shouted to his men.

'That bitch is leading them! She's that freak they think is their Queen. Take her out first.'

As one of his men moved to the radio to relay his orders, Alice moved into the room. She had no weapons with her, but saw a small fire extinguisher behind her on the wall. She picked it up and threw it at the Red Guard who was about to order an attack on the jeep. The extinguisher hit him on the back and he fell from his chair.

Appleseed turned to see what had happened and glared in unadulterated fury as he saw Alice. He reached for the gun at his waist when Alice leapt forward, grabbing the fallen Red Guard's pistol and coming up in a roll behind the console next to Appleseed. He fired two rounds that destroyed a monitor, showering Alice with bits of glass and plastic. Alice saw two Red Guards get up from their chairs and move towards her. Both were reaching for their pistols, but they were communications officers who had never seen close combat before and were just too slow. Alice squeezed off three rounds in quick succession, felling one of them and sending the other diving for cover.

She heard some of the men scream, the despair in their voices clear.

'Sir, they shot down a chopper!'

'The Biters are at the wall!'

The room was suddenly plunged into darkness and Alice heard Appleseed shout to his men.

'Finish her and join me for extraction.'

And then Alice was left in a dark room, facing more than a dozen Red Guards, armed with only a pistol that had eight rounds left in it.

~ * * * ~

Alice heard the Guards fumbling in the dark, shouting to each other in Chinese. She thanked her stars that these were not combat troops and also that they did not seem to have automatic rifles. Even if one of them began spraying with a rifle, life would get very interesting for her. Alice tore a piece of cloth from her shirt and wrapped it around her right hand, grabbing a broken shard of glass. In her left hand was the pistol. The Guards were moving around noisily, perhaps confident that they had her cornered. She stayed glued to where she was sitting, trying not to make any noise. When she sensed movement to her right, she swung her right hand out, feeling the glass bite into something soft. The Guard howled in pain as Alice swept his feet from under him and brought down the glass shard on his body, feeling his blood spurt onto her hands. She then rolled over behind another desk. The explosions outside were bathing the room in occasional flashes of light, and Alice saw two Guards illuminated briefly and fired at them four times. Moving and in near total darkness, she wasn't sure if she put them down, but the shouts of pain she heard told her than she must have scored at least one hit.

Four rounds left.

Alice knew that she could not hope to kill or incapacitate all her opponents. It would be a matter of time before their numbers worked in their favor, so she consciously crawled towards the thin sliver of light showing from the door through which Appleseed had fled. In the darkness, she felt something bump into her, and without looking, she fired two rounds, and heard a man scream. Her muzzle flash had attracted attention and she felt a bullet whistle past her face. She rolled on the ground, firing twice at the muzzle flash of the Guard who had fired at her. She didn't know if she hit him or he was just diving for cover, but she heard the sound of a body hitting the deck.

No bullets left.

The door was now barely ten feet away and Alice got up in a crouch, ready to make a run for it when several bullets pinged off the floor near her. She sat down behind an overturned table as she heard the continuing sounds of the battle outside. The difference was that she could no longer hear the helicopters and the gun turrets were silent- the only sounds were the howling of the Biters, rifles firing on full automatic and the occasional thump of an RPG round hitting home. That would mean the wall must have been breached. She took her pistol and hurled it towards a corner of the room and as it landed, several of the Guards opened fire at it. That gave Alice the window of opportunity she needed, and she sprinted out the door, closing it as she felt bullets impact into it from the other side. She locked the door, and while she knew that the Guards would probably break it down soon enough, at least she would buy herself some time.

She was in a corridor that was illuminated by only a handful of small lights along the ceiling. She couldn't see any doors or windows along the corridor other than a single door at its end. As she heard the Red Guards start to try and break down the door behind her, she ran down the corridor. When she reached the door, she found it unlocked and found a single Red Guard standing on the other side. He turned around, surprised to see anyone inside other than fellow Red Guards. He had an assault rifle in his hand, but before he could bring it up, Alice grabbed the rifle with both hands and brought it up, smashing the butt in the man's face. As he staggered back, Alice reached into the holster on his belt and took out his pistol. By the time the man had recovered enough to charge at her, she fired two rounds at point blank range. The Red Guard went down and did not get up. As eager as she was to go after Appleseed, she realized that blundering on ahead unarmed was going to be sure suicide. So she took a minute to take the Red Guard's rifle, pistol and the belt that held his spare clips. Then she set down the dark corridor. The first thing she noticed were the growling noises coming from both sides.

She picked up a lamp from the wall and shone it around, and saw a row of cells lining the corridor. From several of the cells came moaning or growling sounds, and the whole place had a foul stench. Alice figured this was a prison where Appleseed and the Red Guards kept prisoners and she approached one of the cells, trying to see who was inside.

'Hello, is someone inside?'

A yellowed hand gabbed the bars and a decayed, torn face smashed up against them. Alice was so stunned she fell back as the Biter began beating his head against the bars. The lamp in her hand shattered against the ground, and the room was enveloped in darkness. Biters in several other cells along the corridor began screaming as Alice grabbed her weapons and ran down the corridor, trying to get away as fast as possible. She couldn't figure out why anyone would keep Biters in cells like these, but knowing Appleseed and his masters, she knew that they must not have been up to any good. She saw a stairwell at the end of the corridor and climbed up, opening a small door to the outside. When she stepped out, she found herself on a narrow ledge near the rooftop. She could see Appleseed with two Red Guards on the roof and she heard him shout to one of his men.

'Get on the radio again and ask how far that chopper is.'

Alice leaned over and saw that the battle outside was all but over. Biters were now streaming into the courtyard and mixed with them were men carrying assault rifles and RPGs. She could not be sure in the darkness, but she thought she spotted Satish and a few of his men. As Alice saw them she hoped that more of her friends from Wonderland had survived.

There were still a few pockets of resistance as she saw Red Guards firing from windows, but it was a losing battle given the sheer numbers of Biters who were now rampaging inside and the firepower their human comrades were bringing to bear.

The jeep carrying the Queen was also now entering the courtyard and Alice saw her look up straight at her. Next to the Queen was Bunny Ears.

'Alice!'

The Queen had shouted out to her, obviously relieved at seeing her alive and well, but in doing so she had attracted Appleseed's attention. Alice ducked as a bullet slammed into the bricks behind her and dove onto the rooftop, taking cover behind a water tank. Appleseed was on the other side of the roof and he and his men were now crouched behind a large satellite dish. Both Red Guards had rifles and seemed to know how to use them. Every time Alice tried to lean around the corner of the tank to take a shot, they would lay down a withering fire that had her ducking for cover. She heard a voice that she recognized scream above the din of gunfire and howling.

'Save Alice. She must live!'

It was the Queen.

Alice watched as two black clad men climbed onto the roof, but the Red Guards were in a great defensive position, covered by the large satellite dishes and boxes near them. Both Zeus troopers went down under a steady volley of fire. However that gave Alice time to take aim and fire a quick burst at the two Red Guards, sending them scampering for cover. She leaned out and saw several Biters try and climb up to the roof. Many of them fell in trying to climb the stairs and even when one or two actually made it close to the roof, the Red Guards picked them off one by one, with carefully aimed head shots. When two Biters actually seemed to be about to make it to the top, one of the Red Guards tossed a grenade that obliterated them. Alice heard a helicopter approach, and that galvanized her into action. After all he had done, Appleseed could not be allowed to escape. She leaned out and saw that both Red Guards were now frantically firing at the mass of Biters. While the Biters were having trouble climbing the ladders, two black-clad men were now almost at the roof, and firing at the Red Guards. While both men went down to another grenade rolled at them, they had distracted the Red Guards long enough to not notice the new danger they faced.

A large truck had been driven up along the roof and Biters were launching themselves off its top at the roof. Several fell short, but many made it, and all the while the Queen kept screaming.

'The prophecy must be fulfilled! Alice must live!'

The two Red Guards were now beginning to falter as they realized that there was no way they could hold back the flood of Biters, and they were steadily backing up behind the satellite dishes. Alice caught a glimpse of Appleseed, firing his pistol at the approaching Biters.

Even as Biters fell, more climbed over them, trying to get to the Red Guards. Alice saw that she had a clear shot and fired a burst that caught one of the Red Guards in the shoulder. He fell, screaming in agony, and his comrade now panicked, knowing there was no way he could hold his position alone. That split second of indecision cost them dearly as the Biters were on them, clawing and biting as they screamed for mercy, till they spoke no more. Appleseed raced across the roof, with a speed that belied his bulk, throwing two grenades that scattered the Biters in his path and firing with his pistol as he ran back towards the building. Alice fired but missed as her aim was thrown off by an exploding grenade and saw Appleseed climb back through the door she had used to get to the rooftop. Thinking that Appleseed probably had another escape route planned, she followed him inside. As soon as she had stepped into the darkness, she felt a burning pain in her right thigh as Appleseed plunged a knife into her. He pulled the knife out and then pushed her backwards, sending her falling ten feet to the floor below. Alice landed hard, the wind totally knocked out of her as Appleseed climbed down the stairs. He kicked her pistol away when she tried to reach for it and stood over her.

'You bitch, I should have just gutted you when I had the chance. But it's never too late to set things right.'

He brought his hand up to stab her. Alice saw his shadow move and brought her left leg up in a kick that hit him in the groin, sending him back, doubling over with pain. She could hear him groaning and swearing as she got up and tried to get her bearings. There was moonlight coming in the through the open door above, and as her eyes adjusted, she saw him circling back for another strike. As he lunged towards her, she was ready for him. She grabbed his wrist and turned, using his weight and momentum against him. Appleseed went crashing to the ground as Alice followed through with a kick aimed at his head. Appleseed blocked the kick and twisted her ankle, sending her down again. He got up, rubbing his sore hand and swearing.

'You think you're so tough. I can crush you with my bare hands.'

All of Alice's training came back to her and she made a conscious effort to relax and still her mind. Fight angry and you will make mistakes, and a single mistake can be fatal. That was one of the lessons her instructors had drilled into her, especially given her usually impulsive nature. But now those lessons learnt in classes, and more importantly in several life and death battles in the Deadland saved her life. Appleseed feinted with his right hand and brought his left up in a punch aimed at her throat. Alice saw him telegraph the blow with the slight roll of his left shoulder and she stepped inside his blow, blocking his arm with her right forearm and then using her head to butt him in the nose. As he groaned and stumbled back, she followed with a punch to the solar plexus and then another to Appleseed's already damaged nose. She heard a crunching noise and was sure she broke his nose when he screamed in agony. Appleseed fell back, but in doing so, pushed Alice hard, sending her bouncing off a wall and to the ground.

To her surprise, instead of attacking again, Appleseed ran towards the far door. Alice was on her feet, but with her twisted ankle was not able to move fast enough to catch him before he reached the door.

He turned on a small table lamp and she saw his bloodied face as he glared at her.

'Now rot in Hell with the Biters you love so much.'

He reached over to the wall and pulled a switch. Alice heard a creaking noise as all the cell doors swung open and Appleseed disappeared behind the door. Alice would have followed him except for the fact that now she saw Biters emerge from four of the cells. They all wore collars and were filthy and bloodied. One of them, a large man with one ear missing snarled at her and lunged. Alice rolled out of the way and grabbed the pistol on the ground, coming up in a crouch and drilling him with three rounds, two to the chest and one to the head that dropped him. The other three Biters now charged at her, screaming and howling. She shot one more in the head before she realized that that they were too close for her to get another shot. She ducked under one's outstretched hands and kicked out at the other, sending him down. She rolled across the corridor hoping to put some distance between them and get another shot, when another figure jumped into the fray.

It was the Queen. She was carrying a large axe and brought it down on one of the Biter's necks, and as he stumbled forward, she brought the axe down again on his skull. The last remaining Biter spat at her and lunged forward, swatting her against the wall as Alice fired, hitting the Biter in the leg. The Biter fell down, and Alice rushed to help the Queen.

'Are you okay?'

The Queen smiled, a strange expression given her lifeless eyes.

'Alice, am I glad to see you alive. The prophecy...'

Before she could complete her sentence, the Biter on the ground jumped at Alice and sank his teeth into her leg. She screamed in agony and on reflex shot him in the head. She grabbed her bleeding leg and stared at the Queen in horror.

'Help me!'

The Queen seemed to flounder and then saw the vial around Alice's neck.

'We must use the vaccine now!'

The Queen wrenched the vial from Alice's neck and took out the syringe, pressing the needle deep into Alice's calf but was able to inject only half the contents before Alice spasmed and the needle came out, spraying some of the precious liquid on the floor. Alice felt a burning sensation spread from her legs to her entire body. Her hands were shaking and her vision was blurring. She tried to say something but it felt like there was a giant lump in her throat. The Queen lay Alice on her lap and took the vial and opened it, pouring the remaining contents down Alice's throat.

'Alice, my child. You cannot die or become just another Biter. The prophecy needs you to live, to bring an end to all this suffering.'

Alice felt the liquid flow down her throat and it felt as if her entire body were on fire. She saw the Queen glance up and then she pushed something into Alice's hand. Before Alice could say anything, she saw the Queen's head disappear in a spray of blood. As the Queen's body fell, she dropped Alice to the ground. Alice's head hit the ground hard and through the red mist that clouded her vision she saw someone approaching, a pistol in his hand. Alice screamed as her body spasmed time and again and then went still.

Appleseed had come back into the room, looking for the key card that he must have dropped in his struggle with Alice. He had only one hope now, to hide in the small panic room near the Command Center and hope that he was not discovered till Red Guard reinforcements arrived. When he entered the room, he saw that all the Biters were down but also noted with satisfaction that Alice was down as well. He had spotted the Biter Queen near Alice and had taken her head off with a single shot.

As he came closer, in the dim light he saw Alice's leg twitching and he put a bullet into it. Her leg jerked once and was then moved no more. Appleseed screamed at nobody in particular.

'I got you all, didn't I?'

He took out a small flashlight and began to search among the mangled bodies littering the floor for his key card. He could now hear footsteps on the roof, and he knew he had very limited time. His foot hit something and he looked down to see a charred book clutched in Alice's hand. He stopped, wondering why anyone would be carrying an old children's fairy tale into a battle.

'All that's left of your damn Wonderland is ashes.'

He began to move on when he felt a cold, clammy hand grip his feet. Appleseed froze with fear. One of the Biters was not yet destroyed. He spun around to face the threat when the door above him swing open and Satish and two other men ran in, rifles at the ready. Satish saw Appleseed and fired, grazing him on the shoulder. Appleseed fell to the ground, and his flashlight and pistol both fell from his hands. He clambered to his feet again, trying to find his weapon when cold hands gripped his wrist and twisted it till he screamed in agony as his bones snapped. He managed to free his hand and saw his pistol lying nearby but before he could grab it, he saw a hand reaching for it and raising it towards him in the darkness. Bullet after bullet tore into Appleseed as he fell, not knowing who or what had killed him.

EPILOGUE

Six months later

'COMRADE GENERAL, ARE YOU SURE you want us to land at the forward base?'

Chen glared at the pilot next to him.

'Comrade Colonel, do I take it that your revolutionary fervor is waning in the face of the enemy?'

The pilot blanched and looked away, taking the helicopter into a slight turn as they approached the base near the Deadland. He knew that for all that had changed in the last six months, a mere insinuation from someone like Chen could send him and his family to a labor camp for indoctrination. That, he knew, was a death sentence in all but name.

Chen looked down at the parked APCs and the Red Guards milling about the base and wondered just how long they could keep any meaningful presence in the Deadland. Expressing such thoughts in front of his masters in the Central Committee would be unthinkable, but as a professional military man, he knew the momentum was against them. While he knew his career, and indeed his life, depended on unquestioning obedience to his masters, he also knew that when political masters refused to see battlefield realities, it usually meant that defeat was around the corner. It had begun with the events in the Deadland revolving around that damned Biter Queen and the girl called Alice. The rout of the Red Guard base and Appleseed's death was a minor tactical reverse, but the larger strategic ramifications of those events had been great. The large scale defections among Zeus had meant that the Central Committee had deemed that only frontline Red Guard units be used in the Deadland. That in turn had meant fewer troops for the continuing war in the Americas, where the enemy was making steady progress in its brutal insurgency campaign. But that was a military campaign- one Chen knew how to wage. What had happened in the Deadland was different, and more dangerous. An idea had been born- the idea that humans and Biters could somehow co-exist and that the Central Committee and its masters were behind the catastrophe that had been The Rising. The idea that it was possible to start to recreate civilization without the control of the Central Committee and its Red Guards. That idea had taken root throughout the Deadland and had begun to seep into the cities of the Mainland. That, Chen mused with a bitter smile, had perhaps less to do with ideology and more to do with the choking off of slave labor from the Deadland. When the citizens of Shanghai and Guangzhou were called on to work the farms, they realized the utopia the Central Committee had promised was not quite the same without slave labor from the Deadland to lubricate the wheels of their utopian society. A nascent campaign of resistance had begun, and many of the dangerous messages which had preceded The Rising- calls for freedom, democracy and accountability were once again whispered in the Mainland.

The helicopter landed and Chen stepped out, saluting the Red Guards outside who stood at attention. He singled out the commanding officer, a burly officer whose eyes seemed to be constantly scanning the horizon. Chen had read his dossier- the Major had never been in combat before, but had been a rising star back in Shanghai due to his political connections. The mere fact that officers like him were being shipped out to the Deadland to make up for losses among frontline troops was a clear sign of how the war was going.

'Comrade Major Liang, how is the war progressing?'

The Major snapped to attention, but Chen noticed that he seemed to be on edge.

'Sir, we are carrying on our struggle to liberate the citizens of the Deadland from the tyranny of fear that the Biters impose and the counter-revolutionary ideas of the terrorists.'

Chen smirked. The young officer no doubt had excelled in his political education back in Shanghai. He just wondered how long he would last out here. As Chen sat in the Command Center and was subjected to a briefing containing what he had little doubt were largely fictional figures of losses the unit had inflicted on the enemy, his mind began to wander. He had no wish to be out here, but the Central Committee had decreed that senior officers needed to visit forward bases to bolster morale and no doubt provide photo-ops which would reassure the people back home that things were under control.

He was snapped back to reality when they heard a sentry cry out on the radio.

'Multiple contacts coming in fast.'

Liang was instantly at his command screen where live video from a circling unmanned drone overhead was being streamed. The looting of man-portable SAMs from overrun Red Guard armories and experienced Zeus operators to use them had meant that several drones had been lost in the last few months. As a result, drones were being used for largely static defense, hovering close to bases like this one. Still, it was better than getting no warning at all. Chen peered over Liang's shoulder and saw six jeeps kicking up dust as they approached the base.

Something didn't seem right to Chen. From all he had heard, the enemy was not so stupid as to walk into overwhelming firepower. Liang barked into his radio.

'Get the two gunships in the air. I want them obliterated before they get within RPG range.'

Another display showed the footage from both helicopter gunships as they took off and turned towards the approaching vehicles. The radio crackled with another transmission from the drone operator.

'Sir, I have three more jeeps coming in from the opposite direction.'

Chen had a sinking feeling in his gut. They had two gunships at their base and should theoretically be able to deal with such a threat, but he had heard of too many bases being overrun. Part of him told him to get to his chopper and get out, but he could not abandon his troops when they were under attack. He heard Liang speak in little more than a whisper.

'It's the witch. She rides with them.'

Chen's attention snapped to the display and he saw a close up of one of the jeeps, and standing there was a young woman with her fair hair streaming behind her, her eyes covered by dark glasses. The other jeeps seemed to have only a driver, with the cab behind covered in what appeared to be canvas.

'Sir, she cannot be killed. I have heard so many comrades...'

Chen shut Liang up viciously.

'Comrade Major, you are the ranking officer in charge of this base. Weakness and superstitious babbling will not help your men. Decisive action will.'

Even as Chen said the words, he had to admit that he too felt a stab of irrational fear. It was one thing to fight men who could be killed and to hunt mindless Biters, but it was quite another to fight an enemy who supposedly could not be killed but could fight like the best trained soldier and handle the most sophisticated weaponry. This witch had been leading the enemy to victory after victory and now she seemed to be bearing down on him. Liang was so focused on the jeep carrying the witch that he paid little attention to the three jeeps that the drone had picked up.

'Pilots, fire at will and aim at the third jeep from the left. That's where their leader is'

The drone operator screamed out.

'Sir, those three new jeeps are firing SAMs...'

His transmission was cut short as the screen relaying footage from the drone was filled with static. A second later he heard calls for help from the two gunship pilots who reported multiple SAM trails headed towards them. Chen watched in impotent fury as the gunships tried to evade the incoming missiles, and then their display screens were also replaced by static. Liang seemed to be on the verge of panic having just lost the edge in firepower he had. In his panic and anger, Chen snapped, all trace of civility gone.

'You idiot! Stop staring at those screens. We still have our eyes and our weapons. Come on to the deck and get binoculars.'

Chen walked outside and saw through his binoculars that the jeeps had stopped and all of them had their canvas covers removed, revealing multi-barrel rocket launchers of the sort that were carried underwing by Red Guard helicopter gunships. Chen's lips tightened.

'So that's why they've been reported to be so interested in picking dry the wreckage of the choppers we lose.'

He had no time to admire the ingenuity of the

enemy as one of the jeeps fired. He saw a flash of light and six rockets streaked towards the base. It was an inaccurate weapon, but at such close range, they did not need pinpoint accuracy. Three rockets exploded short of their target, but three arched into the base, exploding in the grounds outside, sending Red Guards scampering for cover. Chen looked down and saw several men lying bloodied after the strike.

Liang was screaming at his men to open fire with the Gatling gun emplacements. Chen shouted at him to shut up.

'Liang, they are out of range. They have clearly thought this through better than you.'

Liang blanched as Chen walked back into the command center, trying to salvage the situation the best he could.

'Order everyone into the underground shelters. They can fire all the rockets they want, but they can't get us there. If they try and close in after that, we still have a fighting chance since they only seem to have a handful of men and we have more than two hundred fully armed soldiers here. Liang, get on the radio and call in an air strike.'

Chen knew that any air strike would be at least fifteen minutes away, but he wanted the men to feel that the initiative still lay with them. That was when one of the guards on the perimeter wall wailed on the radio, the fear in his voice apparent. The words he said robbed Chen of all the fight he had left in him.

'Sir, Biters are coming in from all sides. Hundreds of them just popped up from tunnels! What do we do?'

***

Chen went back to the deck and froze at what he saw. As far as the eye could see, there were Biters walking towards their base. Each wall had a remotely controlled gun turret and he shouted for one of them to open fire. He heard the familiar buzzing sound as the gun turret fired, cutting through the front ranks of the approaching Biters like a scythe, tearing limbs and bodies. He could see some of the undead monsters still try to crawl towards the base as the others behind them stepped over them and continued approaching the base. Just then, two more of the jeeps fired rockets. This time, their aim was better, and most of the rockets slammed into the base. One tore a gaping hole in the front wall, destroying the gun turret, while others hit the inside of the base, and Chen dove for cover as the helicopter he had come in exploded in a giant fireball.

He crawled back inside, feeling the skin on his arm burn from a near miss from shrapnel. Liang was staring at him open-mouthed.

'Sir, they are on the radio.'

Chen heard a female voice on the radio.

'Red Guards, surrender and I guarantee that you will be left alive. Fight us and you will be destroyed without mercy.'

Chen had heard enough stories about other bases that had received similar messages. Some had fought till the end, but others had surrendered to be looted of all their weapons and equipment. The survivors brought back tales of horror that spread further fear and discontent in the Mainland, and uncomfortable questions about the nature of the enemy and the war they were really fighting. The Central Committee had initially reacted the only way it knew how- to sentence the officers and troops to long stints in labor camps to build back their `revolutionary fervor'. But that had only further sucked dry the supply of battle hardened troops. Which is why fools like Liang were now here.

Liang seemed to be on the verge of total panic and grabbed at the holster on his belt.

'Sir, we cannot let those monsters take us!'

Chen sighed. It would sound brave to talk of fighting to the end, but then he saw the frightened faces around him. Young men, many with families back in the Mainland, fighting a war that now had no clear agenda, far away from home, against an enemy whom they had been misled about. General Chen had always been a good Party Man but he could not let these young men be slaughtered for no purpose. He would surrender and take accountability for it, and plead that the soldiers had wanted to fight, but he had overridden them. He knew that he would not survive long in a labor camp, but perhaps it was time he finally did his true duty as an officer- to his men, not to his masters back in the Central Committee.

He grabbed the mike from Liang and spoke, noting the horror in the Major's face.

'I agree, but we will surrender to humans. Ask those monsters to hold back.'

He asked all his men to put their weapons away, and then walked to the deck. He saw that the Biters had indeed stopped and wondered how this witch exercised such control over what were surely mindless brutes and monsters. The jeeps closed in on the base, and he saw black-clad men disembark from them and enter the base, assault rifles at the ready. The witch was among them, her blond hair marking her out from all the others. The black clad men fanned out across the base and gathered the Red Guards outside in a group, herding them into a room where they were locked. Others began to climb to the Command Center.

Chen turned to see the door open and four heavily armed men walk inside. They were all locals, and wore old Zeus uniforms. One of them looked at Chen and whistled.

'I never thought we'd have a General here as our guest. Everyone, get down on your knees and put your hands behind your head.'

Chen nodded to his men and they all complied. He noted that he could not see Liang and wondered where the fool was. Then he looked up and saw the witch enter, flanked by two men wielding shotguns. She seemed little more than a girl, dressed all in black and with her mouth covered by a mask and her eyes obscured by dark sunglasses. She was armed to the teeth, with a shotgun and sniper rifle slung across her back and a pistol and knife at her belt. Tied at her belt was a book. When Chen took a closer look, he noticed that it seemed to be some old children's book. She may not have looked physically imposing, but her very sight made several of the Red Guards break out into sobs of terror, crying for mercy.

She walked towards Chen and motioned for him to stand up.

'General, my men will be clearing out all your weapons and communications equipment. We will leave enough food to last you a day and then leave. I'm sure your reinforcements will be here soon enough.'

She came closer, and Chen found himself involuntarily shrinking back.

'When you get back, do one thing for me. Tell your masters that the Deadland is now free, and we don't want any Red Guards here. Not a single settler will go to your camps and we will continue rebuilding society the way we want.'

Chen saw a blur of movement from the corner of his eye, and the girl saw his reaction, turning just in time to see Liang emerge from a closet, carrying a pistol. He fired a shot at point blank range before two of the black-clad men shredded him with shotgun blasts. Chen watched the girl stagger to the ground and then gasped in horror as she got up, calmly picking at a hole in her torso. There was barely a thin trickle of blood, and a shot that should have killed her did not even seem to faze her. She turned to Chen, pointing at what remained of Liang.

'Tell your other men not to be so stupid. I don't want any unnecessary bloodshed.'

Chen stammered out the words that were

223

paramount on his mind.

'What.....what are you?'

The girl came closer and said in almost a whisper.

'You should remember me, General Chen, and you should have killed me when you had the chance all those months ago.'

Then she removed her glasses and mask and Chen gasped as he looked into her lifeless, yellow eyes and skin that was peeling off in patches from her face. She said her last words to Chen and disappeared with her men.

'My name is Alice Gladwell. They call me the Queen of Wonderland.'

ABOUT THE AUTHOR

Mainak Dhar is a cubicle dweller by day and author by night. His first `published' work was a stapled collection of Maths solutions and poems (he figured nobody would pay for his poems alone) he sold to his classmates in Grade 7, and spent the proceeds on ice cream and comics. He was first published in a more conventional sense at the age of 18 and has since published ten books including the Amazon.com science fiction bestseller Vimana. Learn more about him and contact him at www.mainakdhar.com.

Made in the USA
Lexington, KY
24 September 2013